Cyber Elven

Book 1:

Fading Powers

C.A. Maven

Other Books by Catherine Maven:

- **101 Secrets of Canadian Culture (& Teacher's Workbook)**
- **Small Boobs & Gams (a satire of extreme makeovers)**

Children's Books by Catherine Maven:

- **King Arthur's Kitten** (picture book)
- **Alien Animals Stole Our Alphabet** (rhyming - handwriting & alphabet book)
- **Alien Animals Coloring Book**
- **How to Train Your Puppy:** A READ-it-YOURSELF Guide for KIDS
- **'Magination Molly** (picture book)
- **Bedtime Mindfulness (Questions for Parents & Kids)**
- **Splash Toes Creek** (illustrator & publisher)

My Other Novels:

- **Coyote Summer** (YA novel)
- **Ex-Betty** (science-fiction novel, quarter-finalist for Amazon Breakthrough Authors competition)

DEDICATION

This book is dedicated to my three wonderful sons – Russ, Tim, and Dean – who have always been a source of joy, pride, and deliciously-absurd laughter; to my most excellent step-kids Adriana & James, who have added new richness to my life; to my awesome in-law kids: Bethany, Sheruni & Timothy, with my deepest gratitude for making my kids happy; and to my friends (you know who you are) for helping to keep me sane when the world seems to be going extra-crazy.

I love you all!

ISBN: **978-1-990333-12-5**

Otter-Girl Press

Burlington, Ontario, Canada

https://sleepingcat.wixsite.com/ottergirlpress

Chapter One: Tika

Translucent multi-colored orbs danced a complex pattern in mid-air, while the six-month-old baby in the crib below giggled and cooed with delight. Four elven stood around the crib, watching.

The eldest elf, Xinar, wore a heavy robe of indigo silk that hung to the floor, proof he did not need to engage in manual labor. His fur collar denoted his high rank in society, and the Wizardelf's cap he wore was covered in Hex symbols to warn that his powers were mysterious and beyond an ordinary elf's understanding.

The gray hairs that sprouted from his ears lent dignity and authority to his overall look, but his bushy eyebrows, which waggled when he spoke, made most elven smile behind his back. Other Wizardelven might have trimmed the wild hairs, but Xinar was too proud. It was only because he was a relative that the parentgroup had chosen him as the Elder to approach.

" ... and Tika's maintaining the holo herself, you say?" asked Xinar skeptically. His double-pointed ears were tipped sideways in disbelief as he looked at the infant. "None of you are assisting her? That's impossible!"

The ears of three of Tika's parentgroup immediately folded back in anger. FatherOne, D'inn, was the first to respond.

"Don't be ridiculous, 'Nar," he said, using the familiar form of the Wizardelf's name that was his due as a close relation, and speaking calmly as if he didn't feel the anger his ears showed. "We did not call you here to challenge us, but merely to witness something that has amazed us all."

D'inn wore the traditional clothing of his guild, a potter's blue tunic over a short-sleeved brown shift which kept his powerful arms free for working clay. On his legs were the baggy pantaloons that most elven wore. The projected image of authority was accentuated by his deep voice, which resonated against the smooth, pale walls of the room.

When Xinar's ears remained bent with suspicion, SoulFather K'ah spoke up.

Using the formal title more appropriate to his lack of direct family relationship to the Elder, he said, "Really, Your Lightness, no one would even begin to think of Hex-training an infant ... Still, we worried this might be your reaction. We will leave you alone with her so you may judge for yourself."

MotherOne, Tiriki, jumped in to quickly add, "– and we have told everyone to stay away tonight. We ourselves will go to CenOps to input for guidance while you test her."

Xinar's ears had begun to rotate forward, but suddenly turned back again. "And where will SoulMother Ch'anja be? – in hiding, perhaps?" he asked, his dark eyes fierce.

All three parentgroup' ears fold flat back in anger again, so he quickly withdrew his question, motioning with his long, slim, three-fingered hands for them to calm down. "I'm sorry," he said, "I did not intend to offend you, only to establish Iftrue and bind Iffalse."

"Ch'anja spent the evening at CenOps, Seeking guidance, before we decided to call you here. She is there now, consulting Net for us all," said Tiriki pointedly.

"Good then," Xinar responded, mustering all the dignity and authority he could. "Join her, and Seek for debugging."

Xinar waited in silence as the tiny elfling's parentgroup filed out of the room, their ears twisting sideways from anger into anxiety. Then he turned to watch again the dancing orbs, which glowed with subtle and entrancing colors while they floated above the crib.

He was caught up, watching the orbs dance for a few minutes – it was such an amazing sight that he was loath to discover it false. He realized after a few moments the pattern was not as casual as it might first appear. The nine spheres seemed to be almost randomly orbiting a central, hovering sphere – he felt he almost recognized the meaning of the pattern. It was frustrating not to be able to pinpoint that meaning – like a word caught on the tip of his tongue.

While he watched, his hand dangled into the crib, and his reverie was broken by a sudden strong grip on his baby finger. He looked down at Tika, and was surprised to see her turquoise eyes gazing directly at him with a look, had it been on a grown elf, he would have called amusement.

He shook off the impossible impression – and then hesitated again when he realized she was maintaining the orbs' pattern while she was watching him – multitasking? – at this age??

To quell the fear he felt rising in his belly, he directed his Mind to the orbs, attempting with gentle Authority to take control of them.

This was a simple but powerful Hex; very few adult elven could fight his control over simple holo-objects like this. He had been granted Sup'rvis Authorization many cycles ago at the end of his Apprenticeship, and at this level, he knew he would sense it directly if there had been adult control of the Hex.

He was surprised and a little concerned to find no Othermind; apparently the parentgroup had given him True about the baby's gifts. But as had happened too often in the past few months, he found his Hex failing. He was unable to take over the Hex controlling them. Ashamed at the apparent weakening of his powers, Xinar had not yet consulted the other Wizardelven to see if anyone else was experiencing this problem. At the moment, he was glad no one, not even the parentgroup, was here to witness his humiliation.

The orbs continued their delicate and fascinating dance in front of his eyes, defying his need to seize them. As his confusion turned to

3

frustrated embarrassment, he Sent Hex more strongly, an even higher-order Hex which no ordinary adult in Elfdom could have resisted.

When the only effect the Hex had upon the orbs was to increase the speed and complexity of their motions, he looked once more down at Tika, who held his finger tightly while her tiny limbs thrashed up and down in the apparently-random movements standard among all infants this age.

Tika's eyes were once again on the orbs, as if he had ceased to exist. Xinar noted, however, that she had stopped gurgling with pleasure and now appeared to be concentrating, her tiny copper eyebrows drawn into a frown, delicate ears glowing rosy with effort where they poked out of the soft red down of her hair. When her eyes again met his for an instant, though, she pursed her lips, her tiny pink tongue protruding. Was she blowing a raspberry at him?

With real fear creeping into his Mind, he attempted to throw a full Override Hex at the orbs – then watched in horror as the fragile spheres tumbled out of their safe orbits, shattered against one another, and rained what looked like glass fragments toward the helpless infant, who watched without surprise as the deadly looking shards dropped toward her.

Xinar hesitated a moment too long in panic – he had never been so out of control since Initiation – then gasped out loud as the shards slowed, stopped, and finally dissolved into flower petals which fluttered harmlessly down onto the elfling, who blinked as if surprised, and then cooed with pleasure as the soft objects floated toward her. While the holo-objects could not have actually hurt her, she ought to have been terrified. She very obviously wasn't in the least.

Her tiny hand released its grip on Xinar's finger to grasp clumsily at the petals still falling, attempting to shove them into her toothless mouth and gurgling triumphantly.

Xinar stepped back, double-hearts pounding inside his rib cage as if demanding to be let out. "I am the most powerful Wizardelf in Elfdom," he said aloud. "Am I to be undone by – an infant?"

He experienced a sudden flame of anger, accompanied by the temptation to destroy the elfling, or at least her Mind-power. He could tell her parentgroup something had gone wrong in the testing ... with horror and self-loathing rising in his throat, he tentatively reached out to touch the elfling-Mind – not to harm her of course, merely to test her mental defenses against the day when he might need to protect himself from her, he assured himself ...

... But when he initiated Contact, he found himself awash in the ocean of Net, something he had only before experienced – once – in CenOps. At the time, he had been in meditation, preparing for his final graduation ceremony, and when the deluge of Knowledge, the voices of Net, washed over him like a wave, he had felt his sanity fleeing.

Now, older, more practiced, he tried desperately not to run from the voices, from the Source of all Code and Power ... and felt consciousness leaving him as his Mind refused to submerge, to mingle with infinity ...

His last thought before losing consciousness was wonderment. "... and the elfling lives in this ocean of knowledge and does not drown?"

Chapter Two: Fyr'wall

Tika wandered slowly through the gardens, letting her hands trail through flower blossoms as though through riverwater, trying to calm her angry Mind. In some back part of her Mind, she could hear Teacher Mudlah calling her, but with practiced ease, she blocked the Call. The elfling knew she would later pay for this willfulness with extra chores, but she was frustrated – and tired of being treated like a baby. *'Why can't old Mudlah just answer my question?'* she wondered for the thousandth time. *'It's a simple question. All I want is a simple answer!'*

She stopped when she realized she was just outside the Potter's Guild. FatherOne, D'inn, would be here today for sure. The Summer Festival was coming up, and he always made new and special serving bowls for it. *'I'll just ask him, and if he can't tell me, I'll go back to class and be good,'* she promised herself.

She had to push with all of her strength to open the heavy wooden door, and the noise and pungent smells from inside almost made her turn around and go right back to class, but as soon as she poked her head through the door, FatherOne spotted her.

"Tika!" he smiled. "What a lovely surprise! Come in!"

Tika felt a pang of guilt, because obviously FatherOne didn't know she was supposed to be in school right now. Quickly, she squashed the thought. "Ha, FatherOne," she greeted him politely.

D'inn quickly washed his muddy hands in the sink and then swept her up in his strong arms. "You can call me Pa, even here," he reminded her. "These are all my friends." He kissed her check and then held her up so the other six potters could see her. "Look who's come to visit!"

"Ha, Tika!" they all said, smiling at the little red-haired elfling.

"Shouldn't you be in school?" one of them asked, eyebrows raised.

"Shhh …" warned Pa. "What is this 'school' you speak of?"

Everyone laughed, and Tika realized that Pa had known, but hadn't cared, about her playing hooky. It made her heart light.

He took her into the Guild's kitchen. "Lights," he Sent, and the overhead light came on, illuminating the room in a gentle glow. He poured them both a cup of tea and offered her a plate of cookies. "SoulMother Ch'anja sent these over today," he told her. "She must have known you were coming!"

Tika shook her head, her red curls bouncing around her face. "No, I just decided," she told him.

Pa reached over and squeezed her cheek. "I know, Punkin," he said. "Now, why don't you tell me what I can teach you that you can't learn in school? – Have you decided to Apprentice as a Potter?"

She had a moment of panic before she realized Pa was teasing her. Nobody started Apprenticeship until their sixteenth year. She was skipping school today, but that didn't mean she was ready to stop going!

"No, I came to ask you a question," she admitted. She dunked her cookie in her milky, sugary tea and chewed thoughtfully for a moment while she worked up the courage to tell him what her question was. Patient and wise, Pa didn't press her, just copied her actions, ceremoniously dunking his own cookie before popping the whole thing in his mouth like it was a raspberry, rather than a cookie as big as her whole hand.

"It's just … I asked Teacher Mudlah, and she refuses to answer," explained Tika.

"Oh? What question? You always do ask the most interesting questions!" Pa's raised eyebrows and small smile let her know he understood how she felt about her Teacher.

"I just … She's teaching us to heat water! You know I can do that in my sleep!"

"Hmmm. Well, everyone knows you are very good at

, Tika. But that's not a question, is it?"

"Yes, Pa. I mean, no … Okay. My question is, I know we use our Minds to Command the cookstones, right?"

"Absolutely," Pa agreed.

"So my question is, how do Hexes actually work?"

"Isn't that what they're teaching you in School? … You picture the end result you want, and Send a Hex to make it happen. Magik!"

Tika gave him her stubborn look. "I KNOW that," she said, her bottom lip coming out in a pout as she frowned. "What I WANT to know is, if my Mind can make the cookstones hot, why can't I use my Magik to make my bed warm before I get in?"

"Is your bed cold at night? We can get you another blanket."

"No, no, NO. I don't care about my stupid bed!" Tika had tears in her eyes. Why couldn't the elven around her understand her better? She struggled to think of another way to ask. "I mean … why can't we use our Magik to heat anything we want? Other things that aren't cookstones, or bathtub water, or room heaters?"

Pa rubbed a calloused hand over his chin, and then through his own red hair, kept cut close to his scalp to prevent it catching on fire when the kiln was fully hot. "Hmmm, that IS a good question, Tika. What did Teacher Mudlah tell you?"

"Nothing! She always treats me like an Elfling!" Tika's bottom lip quivered, and Pa struggled to hide his smile.

"Well, Tika, my darling, you are only nine years old," he reminded her gently. He pulled her onto his lap, pulled over her cup of tea, and handed her another cookie. "The truth is, Tika, I don't know the answer to your question. I can tell you that Hexes don't work on most structures, trees or other plants. They only work between us elven, with our farm animals, and with some of the objects inside our buildings."

"Do you think if I learned more Hexes, I could use my Magik to heat anything?" she insisted.

"What's with this desire to heat things?"

She wiggled off his lap and stood between his knees, looking up into his eyes, which regarded her seriously. "It's not about heating things, Pa … It's about why there are limits to Magik."

"Oh, my. That IS a big question, and one I can't answer any more than Teacher Mudlah can," he said, looking sad. "I wish I could answer that, my darling. I know that different elven have different levels of Magik – like you have more natural Magik than I do! – and that only those with Sup'rvis Authorization can do certain Hexes. But as to why there are some things we can't use Magik on, I have no idea. Sorry, Punkin."

He pulled Tika in for a hug. She buried her face in his apron, despite the smell of strange chemicals in it. "Who can tell me, Pa?"

"I know you won't like this answer, but maybe someday, when you're bigger, you'll have Access to Net, and Net may know." He thought about Xinar, and then pushed the thought away. Xinar had never fully recovered from testing Tika, though he refused to say what had happened. But D'inn knew that his tiny elfling had made an enemy that night – an enemy of one of the most powerful Wizardelven in Elfdom. He wanted to protect her, to make her see the danger of asking too many questions – but her curiosity was a big part of who she was, and he didn't want to kill that in her.

Tika stayed tight in his hug, hiding her face so she didn't give away that she already did have Access to Net. Why did everyone assume she didn't? And why didn't everyone Access Net in their minds?

"I have another question," she said instead, looking up from his chest.

He kissed the top of her head and asked patiently, "What is it, my darling?"

"Why doesn't our family have any other elflings? All of the other families have two or three … Is it because I am so strange? Are you and the other members of the parentgroup afraid of making another one like me?" There were tears in her eyes now, and she buried her face in his chest again.

D'inn gently shoved her back so he could look her in the eye. "Tika Tamir, as I said, most of your questions are interesting, but this one is very wrong!" he said, picking her up and holding her on his lap again. "Don't you ever blame yourself for this again, please. The truth is, Tika, that we have tried and tried to have more little elflings – especially ones as AMAZING as you, but it just hasn't happened. It's NOT your fault at ALL! … Are you sad that you don't have little brothers and sisters?"

"Um … sometimes," she said in a small voice. "But when I play at the homes of the other elflings, the little ones can be a bit annoying, actually."

His big booming laugh filled the room, so that even in the next room, several potters glanced up and smiled.

Tika's heart lifted. "Thank you, Pa," she said, "I feel better now."

After her tea was done, Pa took the little elfling over to look at the finished bowls that were lined up on the large, heavy table along the side of the building. "I'm still deciding what colors to use for the Festival bowls," he told her. "Any suggestions?"

She looked up into his eyes, the same turquoise as hers, in surprise. "You want me to choose? Really, really?"

Pa laughed again, his deep voice resonating in Tika's chest. "Of course! You are a very smart little elfling, Tika Tamir. I respect your ideas."

Tika walked slowly along the jars, each with a colored label, which had been lined up in front of the bowls. She was tempted to create a Holo of the bowls that she could then change the colors on. But she had learned that since she was the only person who could create holos outside of CenOps, it made adult elven uncomfortable. So she had to use her eyes. "Well," she said slowly, pointing, "I think one of the colors should be this turquoise, like our eyes. Wouldn't that be pretty?"

Pa reached over and pulled the heavy glass jar of turquoise glaze to one side. "Okay, turquoise for the base color. How about accent colors?"

"Hmmm. I love turquoise and yellow together," said Tika, placing a slender finger on another jar. "That reminds me of summer flowers – the lanai and the butterskips. What do you think?"

"Excellent choice." Pa lifted the butter-yellow jar of glaze and set it down next to the blue-green one. He looked thoughtful. "I like the idea of a garden," he said slowly. "Hey! How about bright pink and orange, like the putti and garji flowers?" He picked up two more jars and placed them beside the other jars.

"Yes, yes, YES!" squeaked Tika. "Perfect!!"

Pa lifted her into another hug, and then carried her over to the front door, which he pulled open before depositing her back on the ground. "Now go straight back to class," he warned. "Tell Teacher Mudlah that I needed your help to decide colors. Then maybe she'll let you out of detention early."

Tika grimaced, her happiness fading as she thought about her upcoming punishment. "Can't you talk to her, Pa?" she begged.

Pa frowned. "I love you, Tika my Punkin, but even I am afraid of Teacher Mudlah." He winked to show her he wasn't, really. "I'm not going to Send to her just so you can get out of your well-earned detention. Now run along. Please?"

"Yes, FatherOne," she said with her saddest voice, giving him her puppy-dog eyes.

"Don't try that with me, little elfling. I invented puppy-dog eyes! Now GO!" Pa laughed. He went back inside and shut the heavy door.

Tika turned and began to walk slowly back toward the school. She meant to go straight back to school. She really did. But she couldn't stop thinking about how pretty the bowls would be with the colors she and Pa had chosen, and almost before she knew it, Tika found herself at the arched doorway of CenOps. On this warm spring day, the door was open, for which Tika was grateful. Door handles were high even for adult elven, and, small for her age, they were almost out of her reach. Why were they placed so high, she wondered? All doorways were taller than the tallest elf, and most windows were above the heads of all elven, as if they all lived in dwellings created by giants. It was another one of those Mysteries no adult elf could explain to her satisfaction.

Today, through the open doorway, she saw a number of elven occupied at the oversized Net booths. The room was bathed in naturally diffused light from a number of skywindows. Glancing around to see if there was a Monitor on duty, Tika crept inside the building.

"Tika Tamir!" barked a powerful voice from behind her. "How many times do I have to tell you that you are not allowed in this building?"

Tika turned, head lowered in a properly respectful manner. Peeking up through her eyelashes, however, she was relieved to confirm the voice belonged to Dorinda, SoulMother Ch'anja's

MotherOne. The Elder elf looked as she always did – beautiful, dignified, and very much in control of herself. Gray-green eyes sparkled with a lively intelligence which belied Dorinda's extreme age, and her white hair was bound with ribbons into a long rope down her back, hanging past her waist.

Dorinda was dressed in the formal garments suited to her role of Monitor. She was wearing a long white robe and a white, wide-brimmed flattop hat tied securely beneath a firm chin. Though frightened at having been caught trespassing once again, Tika was glad it was her favorite grandparent who had caught her. She noted that while the elf's face was stern, her ears were relaxed forward. So, after a few moments of silence to ensure the elder elf that she knew she was in the wrong, Tika dared to lift her head and smile her crooked smile.

"Ha, Grandelf Dorinda!" she exclaimed, flouncing her abundant red curls in a way she knew adult elven found cute. "It's so nice to see you again. You are looking well today. Is that a new hat? How is your garden doing? The likai seem to be more difficult to grow each year, don't they? – And how is Grandelf M're? Is his joint-pain still as bad as at last Festival? I was sorry he was unable to dance. I have always looked forward to his performances, and it will be sad if he cannot dance again, don't you think?"

Dorinda's eyes softened even while her voice remained stern.

"Don't you try your little games with me," she warned her favorite grandelfling. "I understand you far too well to fall for them. You know perfectly well you aren't supposed to be in here until you begin Apprenticeship."

Tika blinked her copper eyelashes furiously as if shocked, but much as she tried to control herself, she knew the blushing of her ears showed her guilt and embarrassment. She quickly decided to resort to a more honest approach.

"Please, Gran?" she begged, ears cocked forward sincerely. "I won't bother anyone, I promise. And I won't stay long; I just need a few millis to do some research. Please?"

Dorinda again tried to deflect the determined young elfling's request.

"Aren't you supposed to be in class right now?" she asked, then cocked her head and appeared to be listening, though the building was silent as always. "Isn't that Teacher Mudlah Calling for you?"

Tika knew better than to lie. Her ears would give her away in a nano, and she didn't want to have her Grandelf angry at her.

"But, Grandelf Dorinda," she pleaded. "They're learning to heat water! I could do that when I was three." She exaggerated a bit. "Please don't make me go back there. Please? I promise, I won't be long, and then I'll go straight back to class, okay?"

Seeing the intense desire in those turquoise eyes, Dorinda knew the battle was over – that it had been over before it began, really. The young elfling had a way of getting whatever she wanted – she always had such good reasons for everything she asked for but shouldn't be allowed.

"Oh, all right," she told Tika, "but use that booth in the corner over there, and don't bother the other Seekers."

"Thank you, Gran!" said Tika with real warmth, throwing her arms around Dorinda's waist and hugging her until the elder elf pushed her away with firm affection. As Dorinda turned to see if anyone was in need of guidance, Tika walked, as sedately as her impatient Mind would allow, to the booth her Grandelf had indicated.

CenOps was one of Tika's favorite places, though it still seemed strange that she never saw another elfling her age in the building. Plants and flowers grew in graceful containers or trailed down white-plastered walls, giving the room a peaceful feeling. Its utter silence, while making some elven nervous, was like food to the young elfling.

In this tranquil setting – so different from the hurried lives of every elf, old and young, that she knew – Tika could fully open to Net. It had taken her years to learn that Net was not herself, and it was only after she had begun School two years previously that Tika had learned that all other elven could only contact Net here at CenOps. She herself had a constant connection to Net, but it was usually muted, as if her Mind had lowered the volume of a music player.

Tika remembered she had nearly drowned in disappointment when Teacher Mudlah informed the class that they would not be allowed into CenOps until after Initiation, which usually began when elveens were sixteen years of age. The seven-year-old elfling had immediately become determined to gain Access.

Luckily, it hadn't taken Tika long to realize that no one guarded the entrance to CenOps, and it wasn't until her third visit that she'd been kicked out by a Monitor. Not easily discouraged, Tika went back nearly every day until the Monitors got tired of shooing her out the door. Tika was glad when Grandelf Dorinda was on duty, though, because she was the easiest to talk into letting her stay.

It was sad that other elven needed CenOps to contact Net, Tika thought as she climbed onto the comfortable stool in the narrow booth. Net was like a friend who was so much smarter than you were, and often able to answer your questions – the kind of questions that caused adult elven to say, "Never mind that, now. You are much too young for such questions. Everything in its time …"

Today, as the pale sun warmed her ears through a skywindow and she was bathed in the sweet fragrance of a nearby orkid, Tika prepared to try once again to penetrate the hopelessly tangled web of Net – to follow a single thread to its source. This was her secret game, a game she could not remember not playing, much the same as she followed rabbit tracks through snow until she discovered the entrance to the burrow, or traced the Lines of Power through the Village by dragging a stick through the dirt.

She had learned that others did not use CenOps as she did – through a direct mental connection to Net. They came here, but had to use the Vee'ar helmet in the booth to Send their Queries to Net. When she asked why they used the helmet, Tika's parentgroup had told her that no one could see or hear the Knowledge they Sought until it appeared on the screen inside the helmet.

Tika didn't like wearing the helmet – it was adjustable, but still, it always hurt her ears. Why hadn't they designed it to fit better? – but she didn't want the other elven in CenOps to suspect she didn't need it. It felt strange and a bit frightening to know how different she was from everyone around her, so Tika never told anyone, not even her parentgroup, that she did not even require a Vee'ar helmet, or even CenOps itself to connect to Net. The only reason she continued to sneak into the place was the connection was so much easier here – like a nearby voice instead of a distant one.

From Net, Tika had already learned that her Village was at one end of a long mountain valley. There were thousands of elven in the Village, but no other Villages in the world. Or so Net said when she asked. To Tika, it didn't seem possible that hers was the only Village, nor that there were no elven who chose to live somewhere else. Tradition said no one ever went over the mountains, but it made sense to Tika that if this valley were between mountains, there must be other valleys between other mountains, and perhaps other Villages in those valleys – no matter how impossible Net said that was.

Tika had also tried to find out where elven had come from – who were the first elven? But Net always said, "Access Denied," which Tika decided meant either Net didn't know or wouldn't say. She hoped when she was older, and was granted adult Authorization on Net, she would be able to learn more. Although every elveen entered

Apprenticeship, very few ever achieved Sup'rvis Authorization such as Xinar or Healer Wyryn had. Tika realized that this meant some Knowledge was unavailable to most elven, but she was determined that she would have no such limit.

Today, she tried to ask her question again. "Query. Why are there limits to Magik?"

"Specify. Whose Magik?"

"ANY Magik. Magik in general."

"Specify which Magik."

Tika sighed in frustration. One of the things about Net she had learned early on was that if you didn't ask a question correctly, you wouldn't get an answer. Net wasn't very smart, Tika thought. "Is there a Hex that would allow me to heat my bed?" she asked finally.

"You could heat cookstones and put them in your bed to warm it."

"No! – I mean, if I have Magik, why can't I use the same Hex anywhere, with any object? Why does it only work with cookstones and bathtub water and room heaters?"

"Access Denied."

Of course. The adult elven didn't know, or wouldn't tell her. Why should Net be any different? She vowed that someday, she would find the answer.

Giving up on that Query, she returned to her Xinar thread. From their first mental battle, which she clearly remembered but never spoke about, she had been afraid of the Elder elf. When he had collapsed beside her crib, she had immediately sensed his Mindthread missing, and Sent an anxious Hex for her parentgroup, who returned, as shocked at her Sending as at the unconscious Elder.

Net remembered every Contact, and so Tika had been attempting to trace all of Xinar's Queries about her. He appeared to have recovered from their encounter but ever since, Xinar's Queries were often directed toward understanding the source of Tika's power. He had unwittingly left behind a thread-trail that the young elfling was determined to follow. Though he had never again tried directly to take over her Mind, or interfere with her Hexes, she felt sure that he was watching her, and not in a friendly way. That made it even more important to keep an eye on his Queries.

With a young elfling's imagination, Tika had learned to create a mental Virch, similar to the one that appeared on the other elven's screens, to aid her Queries. She simply pictured herself within a great room, the Storecottage of all Knowledge. She based her image of the room on CenOps itself, and had been successful in Accessing simple Hexes, such as how to heat cookstones and water, Call other elflings, and other skills most elven had to learn in school. Her search for more advanced knowledge, though, was always thwarted when Tika ran into the Dragon who protected Net, Fyr'wall.

With her usual persistence, Tika was trying again. "Query. Access to Xinar thread."

"Provide authorization code."

This had never happened before. Tika was surprised and frustrated. Net knew perfectly well that she didn't have an authorization code, but it had never asked her for one.

"Um ... I don't have one. Could I please Access the Xinar thread?"

Fyr'wall appeared. "Access code?"

"Ha, Guardian ... Can't YOU please give me Authorization? I beg of your most Powerful Self," she requested politely, her Mindself bowing low before the large, scaly and sarcastic Guardian.

"You, again!" snorted the beast. "Identify. Authorization!" he demanded.

"It is I, Tika Tamir, Elfling One of the D'inn-Tiriki-K'ah-Ch'anja parentgroup," she replied in properly-humble Mindtones. "I seek Knowledge of Xinar's Queries regarding my Self, parameters Sending and Holo-object-manipulation." She waited, keeping her Mindself prostrate, but unable to resist peeking up from beneath thick red eyelashes.

Unfortunately, Fyr'wall was watching her, waiting for impertinence. "Pah!" he shouted in her Mind. "You alien elfling – you are playing games with me. Xinar is RIGHT! You have no Authorization; you have not passed Ceremony; and you are not respectful. Access DENIED!"

Tika's Mindself was used to such barrages, but Fyr'wall had piqued her curiosity with the new word he had added to his usual insults.

"What's an – alien?" she asked.

The ancient reptile appeared startled at the question, for his leathery wings unfolded suddenly, making him seem even larger than before. However, he quickly regained his composure and folded his wings, looking down at her coldly.

"It's an intruder, which is what you are!" thundered the dragon. But intuitively, Tika knew he was lying to her. She filed the word among the dozens of other questions which she had no Authority to ask.

"I will know Iftrue someday," she responded, unable to contain the resentment she felt at being frustrated in her searches.

Fyr'wall sat back on baggy haunches, and stared at her with contempt in his iridescent-gold eyes. Tika slowly unbent herself, and, feeling like she had nothing to lose, approached him. He seemed to grow before her eyes – no, indeed, he really WAS growing – until he filled the cavernous space in front of her.

"Insolent spawn!" Fyr'wall boomed from an immense height. "Leave here at once! – And don't come back until after Ceremony!" One by one, his scales began changing, growing flatter, thicker, and shifting from their usual green-gold to a harsh metallic gray as they formed into an impenetrable wall.

Tika watched as they changed from the ground up. Twice before, she could have sworn the change hadn't reached all the way up – and today, it seemed the wall stopped at treetop height, and she thought she could still see the dragon's eyes glowing faintly in the darkness above. It was hard to tell in Virch, however, because everything could and did change from one moment to another.

"Aw, Guardian, don't be like that," said Tika, though she could sense his Ai withdrawing. Then, mischievousness getting the better of her, she Projected a large pizadisk into her Mindself's hands, holding it in front of her.

"I've got your favorite," she coaxed the apparently-empty wall, "double-cheese ..."

"Well," she added when she got no response, "I'll just leave it here for you, and maybe next time you'll be friendlier to me." She laid the pizadisk beside the wall, and backed away, looking up to see if Fyr'wall were watching from above.

Oddly, in the cold darkness above the scaly wall, she thought she could make out two iridescent gold eyes, and as she withdrew her Sending, she could have sworn one of the eyes winked at her.

* * *

A few minutes later, walking as slowly as she could back toward school and thinking about her encounter with the Guardian, Tika was startled by the sound of an elfling screaming. Instinctively, she ran toward the sound, and came upon a three-year-old elfling lying under a tree, one foot twisted grotesquely to the side.

Before she had a chance to move closer or say a word, however, adult elven arrived simultaneously from a number of directions. Tika recognized one of them as the Wizardelf, Wyryn.

Wyryn went directly to the injured young elfling, quieting his cries by simply placing a hand on his head. Tika knew the Wyryn to be a Healer, for although she had not had occasion to need one herself, Healers were revered by the whole of Elfdom. Relief from pain was the simplest of their skills. The injured elfling had, in fact, been made to sleep almost immediately.

Curiosity overcoming the fear and revulsion she felt when she looked at the twisted foot, Tika crept quietly around the elven to crouch beside the trunk of the tree. She watched as one adult held the elfling's shoulders while Wyryn quickly pulled the twisted ankle straight. Then Wyryn wrapped both hands around the injured spot and closed her eyes.

Tika closed her eyes too, without thinking why she was doing so. She knew Healers somehow used a Hex to heal injuries, but she had no idea how they did it. Still, it seemed a simple idea to picture the injury and then picture the injury healed.

Tika imagined she was seeing through the Healer's eyes – close to the elfling's ankle, and then closer, and closer, until she pictured seeing right through the skin, through the muscles, till she could see the bone.

She was surprised how real it all seemed to her, as if she were actually able to see the injury. There were three bones here, where she would have expected only one – the one she could see at the front of her own leg. Though she had no way of knowing she was seeing rightly, Tika somehow knew she was. She could even see the jagged crack where the largest bone was broken.

Tika was aware of Wyryn's Hex as a kind of hum around the injury, but this didn't satisfy her curiosity. 'A hum doesn't heal a bone,' she thought to herself. It occurred to her she must look more closely. In her Mind's eye, she moved closer until the bone was right in front of her, the crack looming like a great jagged mouth. Tika could see the bones growing toward one another as she watched, and could feel the Hex which drew them together, but it still didn't answer her question.

'Perhaps I need to be seeing smaller things,' Tika guessed, and shrank her Mindself until she saw herself at the mouth of a great canyon. Great white blobs were swarming around the crack, and she had to fight the urge to duck as they went past. She reminded herself that she wasn't actually inside the elfling's leg. That, like her Virch journeys at CenOps, this was not her real self standing here.

'The answer must be in the white blobs,' she reasoned, and as quickly as thought, she dove headfirst into the next blob that passed near her. Inside the blob were strings which she guessed must be connected to the healing process, and she made herself dive into one that swept past her, shrinking even smaller as she did so.

The strings appeared to be made up of units attached together, so Tika dove into a unit, shrinking once more. Inside the unit, she was surprised to see even smaller strings, double-strings twisted around one another with rungs between them, like a ladder all twisted around.

Could she see inside the ladder, she wondered, and wondering, found herself holding onto a rung of the ladder and looking closely at its structure. Not inside, obviously, but close enough to see the components of the ladder. It was highly structured and colorless, but a few rungs up, she noticed a couple of darker pieces, and decided to climb up to investigate.

The Dark Pieces were like nothing Tika had ever seen. Things in nature had mostly-rounded edges and were quite different from one another. Indeed, most of the ladder matched this description. But the dark pieces were more like things elven made – they had square edges and appeared to be identical. The humming Tika had easily identified as coming from the Hex sent by the Healer appeared to be coming from what she named Dark Pieces.

When she got right next to one of them, she could tell the Dark Pieces were covered in tiny veins in what looked like a kind of metal. The veins didn't look like tree branches, though – they were straight and regular and looked, yes, she realized, more like a map.

'What was a map doing inside an elfling's body?' she wondered, but was distracted by another realization. This close, Tika found she could actually hear Wyryn's command – "Heal" – as if she were speaking out loud. At this level, the command seemed to her ridiculously over-simplified – how could the ladder understand this single word? – but the Dark Pieces seemed to be pulling the ladder, and by withdrawing her Mindself back somewhat, Tika saw that the Dark Pieces were in fact directing the strings toward the broken edges of the bone, building both sides toward the middle.

'So Wyryn is controlling the Dark Pieces, which controls the rest?' Tika guessed, and withdrew her Mindself from the young elfling until she felt comfortable opening her eyes once again.

The other elven were gone, except for Wyryn and an elven couple who must be part of the little elfling's parentgroup. None of them appeared to be aware of her. They were all focused on the elfling.

She was able to watch silently while the Healer completed her work and then slowly opened her eyes. Wyryn picked the elfling up, passed her hand over his forehead again, causing him to open his eyes, and then passed the youngster over to his parentgroup.

As the couple walked away carrying the sniffling, but no longer screaming, elfling, Wyryn turned and noticed Tika for the first time. As Tika walked toward her, the Healer smoothed her light blue tunic, brushing away bits of dirt that it had picked up as she knelt to heal the elfling.

She looked up and met Tika's gaze as she approached. Tika noted Wyryn's eyes were such a pale blue as to be almost colorless, and her hair, which was cropped short in the way of Healers, was the palest of blonds. The overall effect wasn't especially attractive, but did, Tika decided, seem somehow right for her role.

"Greetings, Your Lightness," Tika began politely.

The elf looked at her patiently, as if awaiting the questions she could feel bursting to ask themselves. "Greetings, Tika Tamir," said Wyryn. "Aren't you supposed to be in class?" she asked, her eyes glancing meaningfully in the direction of the school.

"Well, yes," Tika admitted, prepared to begin the same explanation as she had given her Grandelf. "It's just that I —"

"No excuses, please," said Wyryn, holding up a pale palm to forestall the lie that was on the tip of Tika's tongue. "I assume you felt you would learn more here with me ... So, what did you learn?"

"I learned how you Command Healing," Tika replied seriously.

Wyryn's smile was unbelieving, as elven's smiles usually were when Tika knew something she shouldn't. "Did you now?" Wyryn asked. "And just how did I Command Healing?"

"You said 'Heal' with your Mind, and that commanded the Dark Pieces which commanded the twisted ladders inside the units inside the strings inside the white blobs which built the bones back together," Tika said in a single breath, watching the Healer's pale eyes grow wider and wider.

"My question is," she rushed on, "what are the Dark Pieces? They cannot come from nature, and I know of no elf who could make something as tiny, tiny, tiny as that — except if they do, how do they make them so small? — and how do they get them to attach to the ladders? – and how do they put them inside us? – and how do they understand your Commands?"

Wyryn looked completely baffled by the barrage. "Slow down, young one," she said. "What 'Dark Pieces' are you talking about?"

"You know," Tika responded impatiently, "attached to the twisted ladders." Her tone let the Healer know Tika expected her to understand.

"I don't know what you're talking about," Wyryn said, her ears folding backward in disapproval. "You are letting your imagination run away with you. When you begin Initiation, and if your Talent lies that direction, you will learn the Ways of Healing, and you will understand. We Heal through Hexes, through Magik, as elven have always done. Making up stories about bits and pieces being 'commanded' will only confuse you. Now run off to class."

Tika felt anger rising in her chest as it always did when elven treated her like an elfling. *'How blind is she?'* Tika thought. She looked up into Wyryn's eyes. They were still kind, she noted, but there was a stubborn denial there. *'How can she be a Healer and not understand Healing?'* she wondered to herself. Tika did not for a moment doubt what she had seen. It was simply another question she must ask of Net, if – no, WHEN – she was granted full Authorization.

Without saying good-bye, then, Tika turned and strode away from the other elf, kicking any stone foolish enough to sit in her path. *'How much longer must I wait to have my questions answered seriously?'* she thought resentfully. *'And how many more times will I scrub floors in payment for my curiosity?'* she added, anger turning to resignation as she re-entered the school to face her Teacher.

Chapter Three: M'raj

Later that day, Tika was once again on her knees, alone in the classroom after school, scrubbing the floor – as she had done on a regular basis ever since she started school. In some ways, she didn't care – she actually preferred a mindless activity like scrubbing floors to the mind-numbing boredom of listening to Teacher explain something as simple as Sending a message!

The boring activity of scrubbing floors also allowed her Mind to wander – which it loved to do. She pictured using Magik to make the scrub brush move. She could clearly picture it, scrubbing and dancing along the floor in time to some festival music. It made her laugh out loud to imagine! She reached out with her Mind to Hex the scrub-brush, but felt – nothing. So many things in her world didn't make sense!

Sighing, she dunked the brush in the bucket and continued to wash the hard way, since there didn't seem to be an easy way.

"Ha, Tika ... Mind if I join you?" said a voice which echoed in the empty classroom.

Tika looked up, surprised. It was one of her classmates – M'raj. Blue-haired M'raj, who had never said a word to her before today, was the biggest elfling in the class and probably the strongest, though she was also super shy and seldom spoke in class. Since she never said much, Tika actually didn't know very much else about her, though she was pretty sure they were actually distant relatives.

"Ha, M'raj. Um ... sure," she said uncertainly, nodding her head toward the bucket. "... but ... Why? – Unless you really enjoy scrubbing?" Tika stuck her tongue out to show she was joking.

The other elfling smiled and went over to the cupboard to get another scrub brush, then returned and kneeled on the other side of the bucket. "Faster with two, right?"

"Um, yeah, for sure," said Tika. "But – are you in Detention, too?"

"Nah, it just makes me mad that every elf is expected to learn at the same speed. That's just stupid," she said quietly.

These were more words than Tika could remember M'raj ever saying, and she was surprised. She thought she was the only one who resented the slow speed of the lessons. "You, too?" she asked.

"Oh, I'm no Tika Tamir," said M'raj with a funny tone. "But my MotherOne, L'la, taught me to Send messages years ago! We're nine, not three!"

Tika laughed, embarrassed at the praise. " … I know. It's so unfair, right?"

"Absolutely," said M'raj. "My SoulFather, J'endo, has spoken to old Mudlah several times, asking her to put me in a more advanced class, but Teacher told him that some of us …" and with this, M'raj pointed her scrub brush at Tika and herself, "… need to learn patience as much as Magik!"

Tika laughed because it was actually true, and then changed the subject because she wasn't learning patience very quickly. "I – didn't even know you could talk," she admitted.

M'raj's face and ears turned bright red, a startling contrast against her cerulean hair and green eyes. "I'm – selectively – mute. If I don't have anything to say, I don't speak," she said hesitantly, as if expecting Tika to judge her.

"Oh," Tika said instead. "That's actually pretty smart. I shoot my mouth off all the time – and get in trouble for it! Maybe I can learn a thing or two from you … So – you're, like, my third cousin or something, aren't you?"

M'raj nodded without looking up. Tika noticed that the other elfling was making much faster progress than she was, and redoubled her efforts. They worked silently for awhile, and soon the floor was finished.

"There!" said M'raj with a satisfied grin. "Eight fingers DO make the work go faster!"

"For sure!" Tika stood, and started to drag the bucket toward the low window. Water was never wasted in the Village, and brown water such as this was to be poured out the window onto the garden outside. Before she'd made it more than a couple of feet, however, the bucket was lifted away from her. M'raj strode over to the window and easily lifted the heavy bucket to toss the water out the window. But just as she was about to let go, the handle of the bucket snagged on her sleeve and the bucket hit her shoulder. Dirty water splashed down the front of her pretty orange tunic and onto the nice clean floor.

Tika really, really tried, but the laughter jumped out of her mouth without her permission. For a moment, M'raj looked angry, and then she put the bucket down and started laughing, too.

They laughed together until their eyes shone with tears. "O-kay," said M'raj finally, patting her wet top. "If you don't mind drying the floor for me, I'll just go to the washroom and try to dry off a bit ..."

Tika nodded, still unable to talk, and then reached inside the cupboard for a floor towel. It had been delightful to have someone help her, especially someone who understood how she felt. But it also felt – strange. She was used to be alone most of the time. What did the bigger elfling want?

M'raj returned just as Tika was hanging the wet towel on a drying rack. "The sun will finish drying me off," M'raj said. "What do you want to do now?"

"Um ... I usually go to CenOps after school," Tika admitted, since everyone already seemed to know that she did this forbidden activity.

"BO-RING!" announced M'raj. "Let's go play Ring-Stick!"

Tika had actually never played Ring-Stick, although it was a common game among elflings. She knew that one player rolled the ring and the other player or players tried to throw the stick through it. She wasn't sure she could do it, but didn't want to say that to M'raj, so she said, "Um … sure, I guess."

"Ringer or Sticker?" M'raj asked after they had retrieved the equipment from the outdoor locker behind the school. They walked over to the circle of hard-packed dirt in the middle of the playground and M'raj held up both pieces, her blue eyebrows raised quizzically.

It took Tika a couple of seconds to understand what the elfling was asking. "Um … Ringer, I guess?"

"Ringer it is," said M'raj. Then she hesitated. "You DO know how to play this, right?"

"Um … in theory … I've never actually played before."

"Really?? … Well, it's pretty easy. Stand at the edge of the circle and roll the ring along that line" – she pointed to a dark line that ran through the center of the dirt circle. "I'll try to toss the stick through it. Okay?"

"I'll try," said Tika. She stood the ring on the ground and gave it a push. It wobbled uncertainly for a couple of feet and fell over.

"Here, let me show you," said M'raj with no malice in her tone. She picked up the ring, swung it backward and then released it suddenly. The ring followed the line across the circle and then fell into the grass on the far side.

"Wow! You're good!" said Tika, impressed. "You make it look easy!"

The other elfling was already striding over to where the ring had fallen. "Okay, why don't you be the Sticker for now? You can watch me toss the ring, and then we'll switch."

"Um … okay," said Tika without much confidence. Throwing the stick didn't seem any easier than rolling the ring. It wasn't, and so it wasn't until M'raj slowed the ring down to barely rolling that Tika was able to throw the stick through.

After a few more instructions, though, Tika got quite good at tossing both ring and stick, and so Tika didn't realize how much time had passed until she heard SoulMother Ch'anja Calling her inside her head.

"I – have to go home for dinner," she told M'raj breathlessly. "But this was awesome! Thank you so much for teaching me – and for helping with the floor!"

Tika found herself swooped into a hug, and after a brief moment of awkwardness, she returned the hug enthusiastically.

"See you in class tomorrow?" asked M'raj as they put the equipment back in the locker. "Or – might you have better things to do?" She winked to show that she was teasing.

Tika put a slender finger to her cheek as if thinking. "Well, I don't have anything special planned, so I MIGHT show up for school," she said, smiling. "See you!"

She ran home, her heart lighter than it had been in a very long time. *I think I've made a friend!* she thought to herself.

Chapter Four: Ring-Stick

"… and I threw it RIGHT through, even when M'raj threw the ring as hard as she could!" Tika finished, pausing only to stuff another mouthful of delicious stew into her mouth.

SoulMother Ch'anja smiled. "I'm glad." she said, glancing around at the rest of the smiling parentgroup. "It's about time you had a friend. And L'la told me that M'raj is only just behind you in the class."

"Really?" Tika couldn't hide her surprise. "She never says a WORD in school!" She hesitated, and then added, "But then, she basically never shut UP once we were playing together. It's like she is two different elflings!"

"Not everyone is willing to challenge Teacher Mudlah," said SoulFather K'ah without smiling. "Not everyone is willing to scrub floors rather than do as she should."

"Sorry, Parentgroup," said Tika, embarrassed. She wanted to say that – once again! – FatherOne D'inn had not been angry at her for skipping school, but she didn't want to get him in trouble.

"Tika actually came to help me choose colors for the Fall Festival bowls," D'inn said calmly, as if reading her mind. "I didn't think it was a big deal."

MotherOne Tiriki glared at D'inn. "I thought we all agreed not to encourage her misbehavior," she said, her mouth pulled down.

Tika felt worse about the strife between her parentgroup than she had about scrubbing floors, so she jumped in, "It's my fault, not Pa's," she said. "He told me to go back to class!" She thought it was probably a good idea not to mention the tea and cookies.

"And then I'm sure your SoulMother Dorinda let her stay in CenOps again!" said Tiriki to Chan'ja, sighing. "How are we supposed to raise a good elfling when everyone gives in to her?"

31

Tika opened her mouth to defend Grandelf Dorinda, and then looked around at the faces of the parentgroup and closed it again. She was in enough trouble already.

K'ah spoke up, ever the peacemaker. "Well, everyone in the Village knows that Tika is special. I think we can't expect her to behave like an ordinary elfling." He leaned down and kissed her forehead. "And I think it's wonderful that she has found a friend! And played Ring-Stick! Do you remember, D'inn? Tiriki was the Champion Ring-Stick player in the whole Village!"

"Yes, said D'inn. "Tika, after dinner, would you like to see the vids of MotherOne Tiriki when she was just a little older than you, killing it at Ring-Stick?"

"Yes, yes, YES!" said Tika. "You played Ring-Stick?" she asked, looking wide-eyed at Tiriki. "I didn't know that! – Maybe we could play together on our next Break Day?"

Tiriki sighed, knowing she was being managed, but then shrugged and smiled. "Of course, Tika, darling. Your other parentgroup members were pretty good, too! – That's how we met, actually. All of us played Ring-Stick together, and then as the years went on – we realized that we were more than teammates."

Tika stared around the table, trying to picture her parentgroup as elflings. "I can't do it," she said. "I can't picture all of you playing Ring-Stick together."

"Then we'll have to show you ALL of the Ring-Stick vids!" said K'ah, laughing and rubbing his hands together. "I'll make popcorn!"

Chapter Five: Xinar

From that day on, Tika and M'raj were inseparable. Tika had learned that M'raj could talk endlessly when they were alone, but almost never said a word when anyone else was present. Tika also found that even though M'raj couldn't Access Net without a helmet, she was just as curious about the limits to Magik, and so she began to smuggle her friend into CenOps with her.

At first, this went okay, despite the initial resistance from the Monitors, including Grandelf Dorinda. Everyone already knew that Tika was absolutely quiet and never needed any help, so they hardly noticed when M'raj took over the booth beside Tika's. Since M'raj was tall for her age, maybe they thought she had passed Initiation. Whatever the reason, the two friends went to CenOps on most days when they weren't playing Ring-Stick or exploring the forest together.

But one day two years later, when they approached the enormous entrance, hand in hand, chatting together without even looking up, they almost ran into the person who was blocking the door.

"Tika! – and – M'raj, isn't it? What do you think you're doing? You know perfectly well that elflings aren't allowed in CenOps!" The boom of Xinar's voice made Tika jump, but she thought fast.

"Greetings, Your Lightness! What a pleasure to see you here today!" she began in her sweetest voice, the one that most adult elven couldn't resist. "Oh! Is this – CenOps?? Oh, I'm sorry. I thought it was the Library." The Library was, in fact, next door, though the two buildings looked nothing alike. Elflings used the quiet building to study or practice their Hexes.

Tika had, of course, been in the Library many times. But the rooms and rooms of empty shelves sent shivers up her spine. *What had those shelves been meant to hold? And why didn't anyone know the answer to that question?*

Xinar wasn't so easily fooled. "You know perfectly well that this is CenOps, Tika Tamir. I have Accessed your records and know that you have been sneaking in here for – YEARS!" He stood with his hands on his hips. His wild grey hair escaping from under his Wizardelf's cap made him look a bit – crazy – to Tika's eyes.

Tika realized that there was no point in hiding the truth. "I have been seeking answers to the loss of Powers in the Village," she admitted. "But Fyr'wall prevents me from Accessing anything useful ... I don't suppose you could grant me Sup'rvis Authorization?" She kept her eyes looking down, her hands together behind her back in the properly-respectful posture, and stood as tall and straight as she could, though she barely came up to his shoulders. She didn't dare glance at M'raj but hoped her friend was slowly backing away from this fight.

"Listen, elfling, who says Powers are failing?" Xinar challenged. "Has your parentgroup said something to you?"

Tika wasn't sure how to respond. *Every elf in the Village knew that people's Hexes were starting to fail sometimes. How could the old Wizardelf be acting like this was news??*

Tika glanced at M'raj', whose eyes were fierce, though she didn't say anything. Tika didn't want to get M'raj in trouble, but she wished her friend would speak up. Since she didn't, Tika said bravely, "Surely, the most powerful Wizardelf in the Village would know that there are some problems with Power?" She waited for the coming explosion – but it didn't happen.

"These are problems for ADULT elven, not elflings who have not even passed Initiation," he said to them without the anger he always directed toward Tika. "Why don't you two elflings just go play?"

Tika couldn't help herself. She realized that she should get M'raj to teach her how to remain silent when silence was the wisest course. Instead, she spoke up again. "Your Lightness, can you please explain why CenOps isn't open to EVERY elf in the Village? Aren't you sending us to school to gain Knowledge? And if you want us to gain Knowledge, then it makes sense that we ALL Access CenOps, doesn't it?"

This was a question the two elflings had struggled with for years, as they had quickly exhausted what they could learn from the limited Net that school had. But Tika surprised herself by being brave enough to ask the Wizardelf directly.

Tika waited for the fury she always seemed to cause in Xinar, but again, his reply was calm, if condescending.

"Good question, Tika," he said, his tone disagreeing with his words. "But – answer me this. How many elven are there in the Village?"

"Um … about three thousand, give or take?" said Tika.

"Good! And how many booths are there in CenOps?"

Tika tried to peek around him to look inside. "Um … about two hundred?" she guessed.

"That's very close. There are two hundred and twenty booths. How would you share Access to such a limited number of booths among three thousand who want Access?"

Tika couldn't believe how patient and reasonable he was sounding. Where was Xinar, and who was this imposter??

She had never actually spoken to Xinar in person before, but had always been aware of his hostility. Maybe she had imagined it? "Well," she said, continuing to speak bravely, "First of all, not everyone would be interested, right? I mean, the Potters, the Gardeners, the Fixits, the Weavers – in fact – maybe MOST elven – aren't all that interested in CenOps. Besides – even if they were, couldn't you just make a schedule that granted Access to all elven who requested it?"

"But – who would teach young elven how to Access Net? We would need dozens more Teachers! No, Tika Tamir, this is a question that has been debated in Council many times over the centuries, and the current system has always turned out to be the best for everyone." His smile was kind, if a bit smug, Tika thought, keeping her head down but watching through lowered lashes.

M'raj, though, suddenly spoke up. "But – what about Gifted elflings – like Tika? Are you seriously telling me that no young elfling has EVER been granted Access before turning sixteen?"

Tika glanced up in surprise, her respectful posture forgotten. *Why hadn't SHE thought to ask this question??* And – M'raj had SPOKEN!

But it was obvious that Xinar's pretense of friendly patience was coming to an end. "You have been spending more time around Tika than is wise!" he said to M'raj, his voice turning harsh. "You are being disrespectful! You must learn patience and to listen to older and wiser elven … At any rate, I have informed that Monitors that they are not, under ANY circumstances, to allow either of you entrance into CenOps again until Initiation."

He turned and looked directly at Tika. "And I spoke with Dorinda Tamir, Tika, and she has agreed with the wisdom of my wishes. Do NOT come here again until you pass Initiation! Now – GO!"

The look he gave Tika frightened her. It was like he would kill her if he could. In fact, she felt a MindTouch from him, and not a gentle one, either. He was throwing a full Override Hex at her!

She closed her eyes, panicking. If he was able to take over her Mind, he could destroy it! *Think, Tika, think!* she told herself. No one had ever attacked her like this, so she didn't know what to do. MindTouches were absolutely forbidden except in emergencies, but that didn't seem to be stopping him. She realized that she only had moments before losing control of her own Mind.

Suddenly, she knew what to do. Standing this close to CenOps made it easy for her to open her Mind fully to Net. She kept opening until the volume of information coming at her wasn't just an ocean, but a – tsunami! She was scaring herself, not just Xinar. Now she understood a bit about why he had fainted when he connected to Net in her Mind as a baby – this was overwhelming! She wasn't sure she could stay on her feet, and there were black spots beginning to dance in her vision.

"Gah!" shouted Xinar, and the MindTouch retreated.

Tika immediately shut off her Access to Net. When she opened her eyes, Xinar was clutching the doorframe to CenOps, his eyes closed, breathing heavily. He gestured without looking up. "Get – OUT!"

M'raj had her arms around Tika, holding her up. "Let's get out of here," she whispered, letting go to take Tika's hand and lead her to sit at a table under the trees outside the Library.

"What a – Borg!" said M'raj after they sat down. "What happened to him?"

"M'raj! Language!" responded Tika, covering her mouth so her friend couldn't see her smile at her use of the bad word. Then her smile faded, and she sat staring down at her hands. What had just happened?? She knew that Xinar wouldn't be telling anyone what she had done, but her heart ached to tell M'raj about what Xinar had done to her.

But then she pictured the look on her friend's face if she said, "Actually, I've always been able to Access Net without CenOps." Quick way to lose a friend! Well, at least it seemed unlikely that Xinar would start any further MindTouches against her.

But – They were also cut off from CenOps!! That was un-accep-table! She knew that HER Access to Net wasn't cut off, but M'raj had just started to learn how to use it. Tika felt like crying. She couldn't tell M'raj her secret – not ever her parentgroup knew. Actually, she realized, Xinar was the only elf in the whole Village who knew about her ability, and apparently, he had never told anyone, not even her parentgroup. It was strange, sharing a secret with an elf who obviously HATED her ...

"So – What's your plan?" M'raj was asking.

Tika brought her mind back to the present. "Plan?"

"You know – how to get back into CenOps ... You aren't going to give UP, are you?"

Tika was silent, unable to look up at her best – her only! – friend. "I – I don't know, M'raj ... That sounded pretty final. I don't want to do anything that would get the Monitors – and especially my Grandelf Dorinda – in trouble.

"Oh," said M'raj. "Yes, that would be bad ... Maybe we can put on disguises – pretend to be Wizardelven!"

Tika looked up, wondering if M'raj had lost her Mind. But the other elfling was smiling broadly, and it made Tika's heart lighter. "Yes," she agreed. "We will be Wizardelf Fyr and Wizardelf Wall!" M'raj hadn't run into Fyr'wall yet, but Tika had described her many interactions with the Guardian, so she knew that M'raj would get her joke.

"Exactly! I'm sure we could come up with a dragon costume! Then the next time Xinar tries to enter CenOps, we'll tell him, "Access DENIED!"

"De-NIED!" echoed Tika, relishing the image. Then she sobered. "There is a Council meeting at the end of the week. Anyone is allowed to speak ... Maybe we should ask them to override Xinar?"

"Um ... Xinar will be there, won't he?"

"Oh … You're right," said Tika. "He'll be all 'Young elflings need to learn patience' and 'Young elflings lack respect!' … Even if he wasn't there, probably nobody will listen to a pair of eleven-year-olds who want special privileges."

"Have you decided which Guild you'll join when we do turn sixteen?" asked M'raj, changing the subject.

"Hmmm," said Tika. "Probably Healer. But I wish I could also be a Potter like my FatherOne, D'inn. Actually, I wish I could join ALL of the Guilds! Why do we have to pick just ONE??"

M'raj started laughing. "Figures – Tika wants EVERYTHING, all at ONCE, NOW."

"Well … yeah," said Tika, shrugging. "How about you?"

"I'm not sure. I think I'd like to be a Monitor someday. I LOVE CenOps! Or – maybe a Baker, like my MotherOne?"

"Oooh, be a Baker! Then I can have all of the blueberry muffins I want!!"

"Okay, my friend, I will choose my entire future based on YOUR muffin addiction." M'raj smiled. "Want to go play Ring-Stick? I mean, it isn't going to solve our CenOps problem, but we can toss the Ring and throw the Stick EXTRA hard!" suggested M'raj.

"I – guess," said Tika, sighing, her mind back on what had just happened. Was Xinar going to block her every step of the way? Would he even ALLOW her to pass Initiation when she turned sixteen? Still, the day was sunny, and it seemed a shame to waste it, so she got up from the seat, took M'raj's hand, and they headed toward the playground.

Chapter Six: The Conversation

The night after Tika's thirteenth birthday, when she was supposed to be asleep, she got up to get some water and overheard a conversation between her parentgroup that scared her badly.

"Did you hear what Xinar said at the last Council meeting?" said SoulMother Ch'anja in a low voice. Tika had been heading for the bathroom but paused at the railing to eavesdrop.

"No," said D'inn. "I try not to listen to Council gossip." The rebuke in his tone was clear, but SoulMother ignored it.

"Don't be so pious, D'inn," MotherOne Tiriki whispered acidly. "Xinar finally admitted to the Council that he was unable to take Control of Tika's Holo when she was a baby!"

Tika lay on her stomach so she could hear, but not be seen from downstairs. This was interesting!

"What??" said D'inn. "The great and powerful Wizardelf, admitting that our tiny elfling had bested him?"

"Now, D'inn," said SoulFather K'ah gently. "You should show more respect. Not only is Xinar High Wizardelf, but he's also your uncle."

Tika knew that K'ah was the peacemaker in the cottage. The other three loved each other, but also liked to squabble and tease. Luckily, they were always brought back together by K'ah. Tika treasured him for his kind ways, but right now, she wanted him to shut up so the others would say more about Xinar. She got her wish.

"K'ah, you know perfectly well that Xinar has always had it in for Tika. I think he would have wiped her Mind if he could have. Even as an elfling, she is more powerful than he will ever be!" whispered Chan'ja proudly.

Tika blushed with such high praise, but her stomach grew tight. They didn't know the HALF of it! – But if she was more powerful than the High Wizardelf, what did that mean?

Chan'ja was speaking again. "It's not just Xinar. Let us all be honest now. All of our powers are fading, aren't they? I have spoken to half the Village, and everyone who dares is saying that their Hexes sometimes fail."

"Don't be dramatic, Chan'ja!" said D'inn. "Do our cookstones not heat? Have you failed to heat your bath?"

Tika heard a sob, and it took all of her willpower not to run down the stairs. But she knew that if they knew she was listening, this conversation would end, and it felt critical for her to know.

"I have failed, many times," whispered Tiriki, and K'ah was quick to echo, "Me, too."

"Something is wrong with Magik. At least, that's what they said in Council last night," said Chan'ja.

"But not for Tika," said D'inn with emphasis. "Why not?"

"Nobody knows, but it's going to come to a head, sooner rather than later," said Chan'ja. "She may be our last Wizardelf – someday … I'm glad she has M'raj … Do you think they'll form part of a parentgroup someday?"

"Chan'ja!!" said all three elven at the same time.

Tika heard a chorus of "Lots of time" and "Cross that bridge" as chairs were scraped back. She scurried back to her bedroom, careful not to step on the squeaky boards in the hallway. She climbed into her high bed, but was unable to sleep. So many things made more sense now! – And some made less sense …

Chapter Seven: Bullies

The first time Tika was bullied had been a couple of years earlier. Skills her classmates learned slowly and clumsily, she mastered almost before they were taught; the mere subject name seemed to link her to Net knowledge, and she knew the whole skill in an instant. What she didn't understand instantly, she quickly learned at CenOps, even with her limited Access. Since being denied entrance inside, she had discovered that she had almost as much connection while sitting against the wall at the back of the building. She now spent many hours sitting on a low stool that she left there. It was a sunny spot, and she always brought some snacks to eat, and a scroll to pretend to read, to cover her secret Access of Net.

While her teachers were impressed and delighted with such an apt pupil, it had turned many of her classmates into enemies before she was old enough to fully understand the word. Whether it was as simple as turning on lights, or as complex as Calling one of the animals in the Village (or even an entire flock of sheep or goats), Tika excelled, even as her Teachers seemed increasingly to stumble.

She could see fear even in her Teachers' eyes; the only elven that now seemed to accept her were M'raj and her own family. And – even then, she saw puzzled concern more often than pride in her family's eyes these days.

And elflings are not always in school, or under an adult's watchful eye, and when a group of elflings had come upon her far from the Village one day, their fear and envy had coalesced into a desire for revenge.

Tika had always been tiny for her age, and the bigger, stronger elflings had been thrilled and a bit terrified, to discover that this usually-powerful elfling was almost helpless once a certain distance from home, her Powers seemingly as weakened as theirs. In the Village, there were Lines of Power most elven could tap into, though Tika knew no one could follow the Lines along their paths as she had secretly done since a small elfling. Once outside the Village, however, only an extreme of emotion, like anger, provided Power for her; and that only seemed to affect weather.

Being essentially good, however, her classmates had done her no real harm that first time, just bounced her around and pushed her down, asserting their superiority for a few minutes. The game might never have been repeated if eleven-year-old Tika hadn't angrily wished a bolt of lightning would strike them all.

No one was more surprised than she was when a black cloud appeared in the clear blue sky over them and a bolt of lightning had destroyed a nearby tree. Then a sudden rain squall drenched them all for mere moments before the cloud broke up and disappeared. Terrified at her Calling a storm from the Weather Sat, the elflings had backed away from her and turned to run home. Later back at the Village, they'd feared the consequences – if she told any adult elven, real trouble would come their way, they had no doubt.

In the odd code of elflinghood, however, Tika had understood she could not expose the elflings to their Elders. She knew, with an elfling's wisdom, that her silence put them in her debt, and she had hoped it would be enough to prevent another incident.

She did, however, rush home that first day to confide her fear, anger and shame to Grandelf Dorinda, her favorite grandelf, without naming names. Dorinda clucked over the torn tunic and gently helped to wash the mud from the elfling's hair and clothes.

Dorinda agreed with Tika's instinct for silence, and held the little elfling while she cried out all of her pent-up feelings. She combed Tika's flaming red curls into a temporary order. But Dorinda knew, as tied and combed and braided as you might think it was, Tika's red hair, like her Mind, refused to be bound, and would pop out with joyful mischief just moments after you thought you had it under control. Still, as loving and wise as Dorinda was, she simply couldn't believe Tika's story of Calling a storm.

"But I did," insisted Tika.

Dorinda smiled that superior smile that adult elven often directed at elflings, which reawakened Tika's anger and frustration.

"No one but a Wizardelf can Call weather, Tika," Dorinda said gently. "No one else's Magik is that strong."

"But I DID," Tika said again, even though she knew it was pointless. Her only witnesses were the elflings she refused to name.

The bullying sessions had been repeated occasionally over the last two years, usually following some session in School where she had excelled far beyond her classmates. Nothing could prevent Tika from exploring away from the Village (especially once she discovered the ancient apple orchard about five miles distant), not even the danger of being pushed around. And so there had been a number of opportunities for equally-adventuresome elflings and elveens to corner their too-talented classmate. This was their revenge, and discovering that strong emotions like fear and anger in Tika provoked lightning or other weather did not deter them in the least.

For almost at once, they'd grasped that while the angry weather made for quite a show, Tika was unwilling or unable to direct lightning against any of them specifically, and the worst they would suffer was wet and cold. This made the game all the more fun, as they provoked their powerful classmate into fresh displays.

Chapter Eight: Calling

'Blaize! M'raj!' Sent fifteen-year-old Tika frantically in her Mind. *'Come quickly! I need you!'* She was far outside the Village on a quest to pick apples to use for the apple pie she was planning to bake, so she didn't have time to See whether Calling her pony and her friend had worked. Five of her classmates pushed her roughly around their circle, slowly drawing together until she was surrounded by foul-smelling, bad-toothed, dirty-haired elveens who had been trying, as usual, to provoke her famous temper.

"C'mon," said Br'on, the leader, swaggering with all the power a seventeen-year-old could muster. Tall for an elf, broad-shouldered and as strong as most adult elven, Br'on was a natural leader. He had curly brown hair down to his shoulders and the downy beginnings of a beard that made him look like one of the Knights in Tika's old storybooks. *But he wasn't acting like a knight!* Tika thought.

"Destroy something!" he sneered at Tika. "We know you can do it! Who hasn't seen it?"

He was, in fact, known as a helpful and intelligent elveen within the Village, Tika thought. *But in the presence of his gang of friends, Br'on became a bully.* His ears were twisted outward in anxiety despite his bold words, she noted with satisfaction as she was pushed down onto the muddy spring ground. She was a couple of years younger than Br'on, but in the same class, and he had appeared to hate her from the moment she joined.

She tried to See Blaize while she was down, to See if help was on the way, but rough hands seized her and she was pulled up only to be pushed around the circle again before again being tripped from behind and falling once more full-length onto the soggy ground. Still, she managed to control her emotions.

"Br'on," whined one of the younger elveens, "It's not working ... She's not even Calling lightning, let alone destroying anything..." Tarak had backed away from the group, and Tika wasn't sure if he was ashamed or just getting bored. Tarak was one of her many dozen cousins – not that it had stopped him from participating in these tormenting sessions in the past – but she was hoping family loyalty was beginning to work on him.

For her part, Tika had been learning to fight them without Magik. So today, while they pushed her around, she twice managed to 'accidentally' strike one or another of the elfling in an eye, or throat, or even more tender spot, all the while appearing helpless and terrified.

"The wise elf," she could hear Grandelf Dorinda's voice echoing in her ear, "does not act rashly. It is only through waiting for one's moment that true triumph is achieved."

'Yeah, right,' Tika thought to the voice in her head, *'You try that when dirty, disgusting elveens are pushing you and your new silk tunic into the mud!'* She glanced down at the cloth woven by MotherOne Tiriki, combining Tika's favorite colors of green and blue in delicate and intricate patterns, now covered in brown.

'Blaize!' she Called again, despite knowing her pony could not hear her from this distance. 'M'raj! Please come!' She could feel tears rising in her eyes, and bit them back, cursing her weakness. She became determined to find out how to Call her pony or her friend from a distance to make sure she was never this helpless again.

Today, she reminded herself that the annoying elflings would eventually tire of the game and determined she would give them neither Magik nor tears for their reward. Maybe, if just once she could control her emotions, they might give up this torment forever.

Meanwhile, Tika's hair had come utterly undone, and the way her long red curls blew around her in the wind, like flames against the setting sun, was one of the things that made the elflings laugh, yet at the same time feel a bit afraid. As Tika stood in the middle of the circle, dirty and out of breath, Br'on unexpectedly wished he had never been so mean to her.

Everyone else suddenly seemed to know it was time to be getting back, too. It was obvious that Tika would neither cry nor bring lightning, and the fun was gone out of the game. Other elflings, like Tarak, were starting to feel ashamed of themselves, for her refusal to fight back made them aware that they were bullies.

It was a tense moment. Br'on, seeing the hesitation in his mates, saw his control being drained away, and his own feelings of shame made him angrier than ever. His ears flattened back against his head.

"May your Hex be bugged!" he cursed at Tika, who turned red at the insult. "May your Hex be lost in the wind!"

Tika opened her mouth to answer him tartly, and then stopped. She stared, shocked, and then pointed over his shoulder into the setting sun. He felt compelled to turn and see what she was looking at. All of the other elflings were staring. One of them had pointed a finger.

"Blaize!" Tika said in a whisper. "M'raj! You Heard! You came!"

The elflings were muttering the pony's and elveen's names, with fear creeping along their spines, making the hair on their arms stand on end and their ears twist sideways in anxiety.

The pony stood atop a low ridge, her plump golden shape outlined against the sinking sun. M'raj sat on her with no saddle or bridle, looking like a wild creature. For a moment, Blaize's mane and tail, long enough to touch the ground, blew around her like lightning against the ruby sky. She stood alertly, searching for the Sender of the Call, for her love and mistress, Tika.

Then, locating her, the pony charged the short distance toward the group of elflings with M'raj clinging to her mane. Up until this moment, Tika had been a too-smart elveen; a wonder, surely, but still an elveen. But today she had done what not even a Wizardelf could have done; and they became as afraid of her as of her pony and her oversized friend.

Never had a Call been sent this far, nor a beast responded, and the group of elveens felt a terror which had nothing to do with sharp hooves. They fled in all directions, scattering like maple keys in a spring storm. Tika watched them disappear with amusement and relief.

"You came!" Tika said when they stopped in front of her, M'raj rolling gratefully off the pony's back and onto her feet. "– But - How??"

"Not sure," said M'raj honestly. "I Heard your call, and when I stepped outside, there was Blaize, waiting for me. She must have jumped the fence to get out! … I thought you must be still in the Village, so I wasn't sure why Blaize was there. But she looked at me in that 'Don't be stupid, get on my back' way, so I did, and then I just held on for dear life while she raced out here. I had no idea where we were going, or why!" She wrapped Tika in an enormous hug. "I'm just glad you're all right!"

Once they were done hugging, Tika happily started petting Blaize's velvet-soft muzzle with adoration and gratitude – not thinking, for the moment, about the magnitude of what she had just accomplished.

The pony merely shoved her muzzle into the elveen's armpit affectionately, and then tipped down to sniff the pockets of Tika's tunic, which, as usual, contained a treat.

When Tika was slow to take the hint, the pony butted her head against Tika's hip, almost sending the elfling once more into the mud. Startled out of her reverie, Tika stumbled, caught herself, realized what the pony wanted, and reached into the pocket to withdraw the now mud-covered apple she had picked this morning. She reached down to wipe the fruit on a patch of clean grass, and then offered it to her pony on her open palm. Even a beloved pet could bite elveen fingers accidentally!

While Blaize contentedly crunched the shiny fruit, unaware that she had been involved in any sort of miracle, Tika stroked the pony's neck and wondered what her successful Sending meant. It was a question for Net, truly, but she was too tired and upset to focus, even if she had been able to Access Net this far from the Village. So she grabbed a handful of the mare's blond mane, pulled herself onto the pony's back, and said, "C'mon, M'raj, climb on."

M'raj laughed. "No, thank you, one bareback ride on Blaize is more than enough for today. I think I'll just walk home." She didn't mention that Blaize wasn't really big enough to carry both of them.

"Are you sure?" asked Tika. "It's a long walk …"

"Absolutely sure," said M'raj. "You go on home and get cleaned up. I'll see you a bit later."

Nodding, Tika clamped her thighs tightly around Blaize's belly and Willed the pony to turn and gallop home.

She did not need to direct Blaize, she knew, and felt a small satisfaction in knowing the bullies would take much longer to walk all the way back to the Village. She felt her heart lighten and tears well once more into her eyes when she saw her own cottage, its brightly lit windows casting yellow light into the gathering darkness like a beacon.

Tika was confused and a bit annoyed at her unexpected tears, but she knew these were tears of joy and comfort, and she let them roll down her cheeks to drop soundlessly onto the mare's back.

At the stable, she let SoulFather K'ah take the pony from her, stilling his questions over her bedraggled appearance with a tiny shake of her head. Hurrying on in an attempt to shake off a growing feeling of panic, Tika found herself at Grandelf Dorinda's door. She wanted nothing more than to climb into the senior elf's lap like a little elfling, rather than the nearly adult elf she was. Then she remembered that the old elf was gone forever. But she needed grandelf energy right now!

She hesitated, and then turned, left the yard and headed for Healer Wyryn's cottage. After their odd beginning, the two had become closer and closer. This evening, Tika knew that, as much as her parentgroup loved her, only Wizardelf Wyryn would understand her feelings about what had just happened, even when it was more than she herself could do. Wyryn was the one elf in the entire community who had never seemed bothered by Tika's Powers. Although she had disbelieved everything the elfling had said about the Healing when they first met, Wyryn was old enough, and wise enough, to listen rather than simply judge and dismiss her.

Now, when Wyryn opened the door, the sight that greeted her brought both a frown and a smile to her face before she could suppress them – an elveen in the process of becoming an adult elf, covered in mud from head to foot and as wild-eyed as a pony in a storm.

"Is it advice you would like, or a bath?" Wyryn asked as she ushered Tika into the cottage. "SoulMother M'lina, your favorite elveen's here for a visit, come and see!" she called from the front room.

M'lina entered the room and was instantly hugging the Tika against her chest.

"My poor wee elveen, what's happened to you? – Don't just stand there, you daft Elf," she commanded the one of the most powerful elven in Elfdom, "Heat the cookstones and fill the tub!"

These were common Hexes even an elfling could do, but Wyryn showed no resentment at being given orders. She simply Sent heat into the cookstone, and Sent water to the bathing tub, which filled and began to heat itself instantly.

By the time the old elf had bustled Tika into the bathing room, gotten her muddied clothes off, and assured the elveen her new tunic would be as good as new once laundered, the tub was steaming with warmth. Tika climbed in gratefully, allowing M'lina to wash her long hair while she soaked away her anger.

When the two emerged some time later, Tika was clad in one of M'lina's old gowns, which was hopelessly big but tied resourcefully around her waist with a cord.

In the meantime, Wyryn had Broadcast a Question to discover what the mystery was about, and had actually had time to talk with the one elfling who had had the courage to respond to the Questioning.

It had been Br'on himself. He might have his bullying moments, but he also had honor, and knew a story such as this would come out sooner or later, and he would only look the worse for hiding it.

So Tika found she didn't have to tell her tale; that Wyryn already knew about the gang of elflings, as well as about Blaize's miraculous appearance. Wyryn didn't even question Tika about it, though, sensing her exhaustion.

All she did was Send to Tika's parentgroup to let them know their elveen was safe and sound, and then helped M'lina tuck her into the bed that had once belonged to their own elfling, now dead these many years.

As Tika drifted off to asleep, she Queried Net about such Power of Sending. 'Access Denied,' came the response, as expected. Before she could even feel resentful, though, exhaustion overtook her curiosity, and she slid unresistingly into the peace of slumber.

After she had gone to sleep, the two Elder elven found themselves sitting companionably across from one another in front of the fireplace. But though they sipped their rosehip tea, they did not look into one another's eyes for a very long time. Instead, both watched the fire's glow, allowing each to think their private thoughts before putting words to feelings.

In the end, it was M'lina who spoke. "I suppose it's time for Apprenticeship, then," she suggested in a neutral voice, careful not to sound like she was giving advice to her powerful partner.

And Wyryn, careful not to sound as if she had just been thinking the same thing, said, "Oh? ... Well, yes, I guess it is."

Chapter Nine: Ceremony

Tika stood shivering in the tiny room, lit only by glitters of colored light from all sides. Her tremors did not come entirely from the cold, although the room temperature was well below normal. She lifted a corner of her Vee'ar helmet to glance up at the elveens who stood beside her, their own helmets unmoving on their heads, as if to rebuke for her lack of proper attention.

'How can they stand there so calmly?' she wondered to herself. 'Here we are, Standing Ceremony for Graduation. M'raj and I only began Apprenticeship a week ago and shouldn't be graduating for five more years. Moog has only been an Apprentice for three years. Doesn't this seem odd to him, too?'

If it did, Moog wasn't showing it. He stood tall and proud. He was well aware of the younger elveens standing beside him, shivering in their white tunics. Even at fifteen, M'raj was as tall as he was, but Tika's head barely reached his shoulders, even with the helmet. Before he had donned the Vee'ar, he had had a chance to get a close look at Tika, whom he'd only known distantly until today. Her turquoise eyes were intensely bright, her red hair was already springing loose from the bun SoulMother Ch'anja had wound it into, and her nose was as small as a baby's. None of these helped her look mature enough for such an honor.

He couldn't help feeling resentful at Standing Ceremony with a pair of fifteen-year-old elveens – three years younger than he was – no matter how amazing their powers were supposed to be. Rumor said that Tika had actually Sent a message across five miles!! Impossible … or was it? But what qualified M'raj? Just because she was Tika's only friend did not mean she was ready to become a Wizardelf!

Moog had always been something of a wonder himself, but he wasn't sure why ANY of them had been selected from many dozens of students to be promoted in this way. Although he was controlling his feelings, he knew that all of them were confused at being Invited to Graduation without the full training normally required of Apprentices. In fact, he was somewhat afraid. The general weakening of Powers in the Village was well known, and must surely be the reason for breaking a centuries-old tradition. Though he kept his face stoic, he sighed inwardly, wishing Ceremony would soon begin.

They didn't have to wait long. From the apparently-random light patterns which had filled the screen inside their helmets, the image of Fyr'wall appeared.

"Ahhhh!"

Tika heard Moog scream. She took off her helmet and looked at him. His helmet was in his hands, which were shaking. M'raj had also taken off her helmet to see what was happening.

"I – uh – there's a MONSTER on my screen!" Moog said, his ears twisted sideways in anxiety.

"Oh, that's just the Net Guardian, Fyr'wall," said Tika, trying hard not to smile.

"G – Guardian? – You mean, it's SUPPOSED to be there?"

"Yes." Tika was surprised Moog hadn't run into the snarky dragon yet. Hadn't he been an Apprentice for three years? What was he doing in CenOps, day after day? "Don't worry, he's actually a good guy," she assured him. "Let's go back in and finish this, okay?"

M'raj nodded and put her helmet back on. Moog looked scared, but put his on, too.

When Tika saw Fyr'wall again, she actually relaxed a little. Remembering the many hours she had spent playing T'tris with the Guardian brought a smile to her face, which she immediately replaced with a more appropriately sober expression.

After examining the Apprentices for a full minute in silence, the dragon spoke. "Who requests Sup'rvis Authorization for these elven?" he intoned in his most formal voice.

None of the initiates was aware of the furor Wyryn's request had caused a week earlier. Led by Xinar, many of the Elders strongly resisted the idea that these elveens might help provide a solution to the general weakening of Power.

"You have lost your Mind!" Xinar had roared at the Council meeting where Wyryn had proposed promoting Tika, M'raj and Moog to Sup'rvis Authorization. "If the oldest and wisest elven cannot solve this problem, what makes you think that elveens can do so?"

"You must have heard that Tika was able to Call her pony from five miles outside the Village?" Wyryn responded. "And there are rumors that she can control the weather, too!"

"Nonsense. You have a soft spot for that elveen. I think she's dangerous!"

"We don't have time to argue," said another Elder, M'rn. "Many elven cannot heat their cookstones. Your Lightness Wyryn, is it true that Healing is starting to fail as well?"

Wyryn blushed bright red, but raised her hand to silence her assistant, E'lak, who had risen from his seat in anger. "Yes and no," she said. "We are still able to heal, but it's taking longer and longer, and leaves our Healers more and more exhausted. All the more reason to seek new Answers!"

The debate had raged for hours, but at the Vote, Wyryn's proposal had passed by a slim margin. Xinar and several of his apprentices had stormed out of the Council Hall when the results were tallied. Wyryn worried that his hatred of Tika made him a danger to her.

Today, unaware of the narrow victory that had led them here, the three elveens waited for someone to respond to Fyr'wall's question.

Normally, as High Elf, Xinar oversaw Ceremony, but he had steadfastly refused to have anything to do with it. So it was the disembodied voice of Wyryn that came from the darkness around them. It sounded as though she was in the chamber with them, though her wide girth would have made the tiny room seem even smaller if she had actually been there.

"I, Wyryn, request Sup'rvis Authorization to be granted to these Apprentices – Moog Moe'bis, Elf Six of the G'lin-Parda-Nur'in-Kli parentgroup, Apprenticed to the Fixit Guild. M'raj Al'bani, Elf Four of the L'la-Sh'een-Werek- J'endo parentgroup, Apprenticed to the Monitors Guild, and Tika Tamir, Elf One of the D'inn-Tiriki-K'ah-Ch'anja parentgroup, Apprenticed to the – Healers Guild," she intoned solemnly.

The formality of the moment was lost as the dragon's eyebrows, which glowed like embers above his golden eyes, raised almost up to his tufted ears.

"Tika? You? You dare Stand Ceremony one week after Initiation? And Moog? M'raj'? Have we met?" Without waiting for an answer, the dragon's eyes refocused into the darkness behind the Initiates.

"Wyryn! Is this some manner of a joke? A new Game perhaps? Are you Scanning to See if I have lost my faculties or forgotten my Role?" Fyr'wall growled with obvious irritation. "If it is a test, I will forgive you. If it is a joke, I must inform you, I am not amused."

"It is neither test nor joke," said Wyryn wearily. "The weakening of Powers has reached dangerous proportions. There are elven who cannot Heat cookstones, and others who cannot Call their flocks home at night … Healing is taking longer and longer."

"I already know this," answered the dragon impatiently. "How can untrained Apprentices assist us?"

All three of the Initiates were shocked to hear the dragon acknowledge the community's weakness. Moog knew of Fyr'wall only from rumors and the scary night-stories of growing elflings. He had heard the Guardian was a fearsome opponent who had never failed to protect Net. Nobody had ever told him the Guardian was a DRAGON! M'raj had, of course, heard lots about Fyr'wall, but to see him in front of her was SCARIER than Tika had warned.

Tika was shocked for a different reason. While she had achieved a level of friendship with the Guardian, he had continued to mock her attempts to penetrate beyond a certain Level of Net, and she had grown accustomed to thinking of him as omnipotent.

"As far as we Wizardelven know, these young elveens are our best chance," replied the voice of Wyryn, sounding distressed and perhaps even embarrassed. "All three have demonstrated an unusual level and depth of Power, and can perhaps See solutions where we have so far failed. We have assembled them as a Team to work together on this problem."

"How so?" challenged Fyr'wall.

"Well, I think you already know Tika, but you might not have heard that she was able to Send to her pony and to her friend M'raj from five miles way …"

"Really? Nobod – I mean … that's interesting," said the dragon. "And the others?"

"Moog is the most talented Apprentice in the Fixit Guild," said Wyryn. "If, as Tika seems to think, the problem is elf-made rather than simply Magikal, he may have the ingenuity and skills to fix it. Despite his youth, he has repeatedly solved problems that stumped the Elders of his Guild … Finally, M'raj is second only to Tika in her abilities. She has shown great aptitude for Magik, no weakening in her Powers, and perhaps most important of all, she is a calm thinker who may help control our impulsive elveen Tika."

"Hmmm ... I will need millis to consider," replied the Guardian. "Please wait."

M'raj was grateful that the helmet covered her face as she blushed deeply. No Teacher had ever praised her in this way. In fact, she was more used to hearing, 'M'raj has great potential, but she is so shy, she may never realize all that she is capable of.' She had always been in Tika's shadow – kind of funny, given that it would take TWO of Tika to actually produce enough shadow to cover her!

Moog felt what had been proposed settling onto his shoulders like a burden. He unconsciously slumped slightly under its weight. Until he had been Chosen for Graduation, he had planned a quiet and predictable life. He did not like excitement! There were many Guilds, and he had decided to focus on the rather mundane skill of Fixit. He had a natural talent for it, actually, he acknowledged to himself, and had been mostly unaffected by the weakening others complained about on a daily basis lately. But solving problems? Particularly those as large as the loss of Power in the entire Village?

Tika was bursting with questions, and found it hard to continue to stand meekly still. She couldn't stop her fingers from dancing impatiently against her thighs, and she hoped the darkness covered this lack of Control. If this was her Challenge, she was ready for it – and even anxious to begin.

Before the elveens' worries could grow any larger, Fyr'wall appeared before them once more, his dragon's face severe.

"This is without algorithm," he pronounced. "I have no protocol for making such a decision. However," he added, looking at each Apprentice in turn, "my Ai was designed to be flexible. Given the parameters, I see no better alternative than to grant Sup'rvis Authorization to the three of you immediately."

His golden eyes seemed to glow brighter as he again looked past them into the darkness. "Level, Your Lightness?"

Wyryn's voice quavered, sounding weary to Tika's sensitive ears. "Full Access, I would say . . . no point in trying to solve a problem without complete Knowledge."

"Agreed," said Fyr'wall in a voice that seemed to be inexplicably sad. He turned his golden eyes upon Tika. Suddenly inside her helmet, she heard Fyr'wall's quiet voice. "Your Access Code will be 'Tika 97114B4'," Fyr'wall said to her. Then he was silent, but Tika assumed he was giving M'raj and Moog their codes, too. Finally, his voice resonated in the chamber for all of them again. "Memorize your Code, for I will not tell you again. Do you know it?"

"Yes, Guardian," the three elveens replied at the same time, as they'd been instructed to do.

"Good," Fyr'wall said. "Tell no one your Code. Guard it with your life. It is Done, then. You are now a Wizardelven, but more importantly, you are a Team. You must stand by one another, for no elven in history have been granted Access at your young ages."

He hesitated, and then his face was on the screen inside Tika's helmet. "Goodbye, elveen," he said, his bright golden eyes shining. "It seems you've gotten past me after all."

Tika looked at the Guardian, puzzled. "Goodbye?" she asked.

"I am the Guardian," responded the dragon slowly. "Now that you have full Access, I have no reason to interact with you beyond recognition of your Code."

"Must it be so?" Tika asked anxiously, tears welling into her eyes in a most un-Wizardelf way. "Can you not be my Guide into Net?"

Wyryn must have been listening in because her voice interrupted whatever response Fyr'wall might have made. "It's a good idea, Guardian," she said quickly, as if to forestall objections. "These Apprentices lack training – they will need your help to penetrate the mysteries of Net."

For a moment, the dragon looked as happy as Tika had ever seen him. Then his face became stern once more as he seemed to recall his role.

"Yes, even with full Access, these three will need guidance," he said in properly-formal tones." I will Guide as well as Guard ... It is fortunate my Ai can be flexible about my Duties."

Had she been alone with him in Net, Tika's MindSelf would have hugged the scaly creature. As it was, she was grinning from ear to ear. She shifted from foot to foot in her impatience to begin. Things were finally going to get interesting!

Wyryn ended Ceremony in the traditional way.

"We, the Senior Wizardelven, thank you, Guardian, for your protection of our Intelligence." She waited for the Apprentices to complete their parts, as they had been coached to do over the past few hours.

"I, Wizardelf Moog Moe'bis, Elf Six of the G'lor-Parda-Nur'in-Kli parentgroup, thank you, Guardian, for granting me Sup'rvis Authorization," said Moog in his most serious voice.

"I, Wizardelf Tika Tamir, Elf One of the D'inn-Tiriki-K'ah-Ch'anja parentgroup, thank you, Guardian, for granting me Sup'rvis Authorization," Tika said in equally-formal tones..

"I, Wizardelf M'raj Al'bani, Elf Four of the L'la-Sh'een-Werek-J'endo parentgroup, thank you, Guardian, for granting me Sup'rvis Authorization," whispered M'raj with a feeling of awe and disbelief. SHE was a WIZARDELF??

As soon as these words had been spoken, the image of Fyr'wall faded away. Tika could have sworn he'd once again winked at her as he left. As the three elveens removed their helmets, the lights in the chamber returned to their normal daylight level, and the newly-appointed Wizardelven found themselves in the plain white room they'd entered such a short time before.

Back in sunlight a moment later, the three new Wizardelven finally had the chance to introduce themselves.

"So – you're the famous Tika Tamir," said Moog, smiling. He turned to M'raj. "And you're M'raj. Nice to meet you. I guess you already know Tika, hunh?"

When M'raj stood helplessly, looking at the ground rather than at Moog, Tika intervened. "Nice to meet you, Moog," she said politely. "Um … M'raj doesn't usually speak."

"Oh?" He was staring at the elveen with interest rather than judgment. "Selective mutism?"

M'raj nodded silently. They all stood awkwardly for a moment before being greeted by Wyryn and six other Wizardelven, who were waiting for them outside CenOps. The elder elven helped the elveens put on the long indigo robes which reflected their new status.

Then Tika finally dared to look fully at her new partner – Moog, his name was. It seemed unbelievable that a mere week before, she had started what she'd thought would be many years of Apprenticeship. She could hardly believe that she was now in some way bound to this elveen she had never spoken to beyond a word or two exchanged at Festivals.

She looked him over critically, as he stood, ears alert, his eyes fixed in the distance, apparently lost in thought. Possessing hair more brilliant orange than her own coppery-red, and wide eyes of pale skyblue, he ought to have looked much the same as most other elven. But on Moog, freckles formed a mask across the center of his face – the sort of mask one wore at Carnival – and tufts of orange hair had sprouted from his eartips decades before they should have. Add to this

his orange eyebrows, which curled and grew like brambles above his golden eyes, and the young elf looked more clownish than Wizardlike.

Still, Tika thought, his eyes and the set of his mouth were kind, and his physique pleasant, if somewhat on the thin side. Not the worst possible companion, by any means, she summed up. She hoped he would find her acceptable as well.

Moog was also sizing up his teammates as if seeing them for the first time. Tika came barely to his shoulders and, despite the somber indigo robe of a Wizardelf, managed to look more like an elfling than an Elder. Her reputation for stubborn disobedience was something every elf had heard of, and he sighed inwardly, wondering how difficult she would be to work with.

Blue-haired M'raj was a cipher to him. She was the biggest elveen he had ever met. She looked like she could pick him up and break him over her knee! She hadn't spoken since the Ceremony, but he knew that she and Tika were best friends. He wondered if he was going to get a fair shake in their newly-created Team. In any dispute, it seemed likely that they would gang up on him to get their way.

M'raj was grateful to have an excuse to stay by Tika. She wasn't sure what to think of Moog. He looked like a clown, but if he had been singled out, as SHE had, to be part of the Team tasked with solving the fading of Powers, he must be special. As always, she decided to wait and see what he was like instead of jumping to conclusions.

They had no more time to think about each other, however, as Xinar and a group of five other Wizardelven approached them.

"Greetings, my colleagues," said Wyryn. Before she could continue her formal greeting, however, one of the newly arrived Wizardelven spoke up. Surprisingly, it wasn't Xinar. Perhaps he knew that what had to be said looked better coming from someone other than him, since he had already clearly and forcibly expressed his reservations.

"I really must object," said an elf Tika recognized as Diro, the Wizardelf in charge of Fixit. "Moog shows a lot of natural talent, and although this seems rushed, I think he will do fine as a Wizardelf. And M'raj is talented in Magik and wise beyond her years. This elveen, though," Diro continued, his piercing green-hazel gaze pinning Tika to the spot like an insect, "is far too young, and too willful, to be given full privileges. She's a danger to all of us, including herself." His white beard was trimmed close to his chin, without a single hair out of place.

Tika imagined even his own facial hairs must fear his wrath. Still, she met his gaze evenly. Two things the bullying sessions had done for Tika were to teach her to recognize a bully when she met one and to stand her ground in the face of opposition.

Wyryn responded. "Everyone here should remember, Diro, that Tika has been Accessing Net since she was a small elfling. Fyr'wall has documented thousands of Queries, most of which he was not Authorized to answer. Few of us, even at our advanced ages, have as much experience Accessing Net as Tika does. While I agree the elveen is impulsive, I think we are in dire need of her help."

"Nonsense! –" began Diro, but Wyryn interrupted.

"Please," said Wyryn to Xinar and the others, who were staring at the young elveens as if they were ready to fight, their ears folded backward in anger. "We discussed this yesterday. We voted. We made our decision, and I suggest we stick with it. We need the help of these elven, no matter what our personal feelings on the matter might be." She glanced around, looking for support.

"Agreed," said Moffa, one of the youngest Wizardelven. She was only slightly taller than Tika, and perhaps six years older. Her blond hair was braided and then twisted into a knot at the back of her head, and her brown eyes sparkled with intelligence and humor.

"You would agree," complained Pilk, whose skin was ebony-dark and deeply inset with wrinkles that were the badges of his centuries of life. He turned to face the tiny Moffa. "You're practically still an elveen yourself. But I also agree, if for different reasons." He looked at the group from beneath heavy eyebrows. "If we could have solved the loss of Power ourselves, we would have done so years ago. It has reached a critical level, as we all know. So, if there is ANY possibility that these brilliant young elven can help us, I think we must allow it."

This silenced any further argument, Tika noted with gratitude. She did not want to have her Authorization taken away from her the moment it had been granted. She could hardly wait to dive into Net at a level that had always been denied her. She glanced over at Moog to see if he felt the same way.

"Thank you, my fellow Wizardelven," Moog was saying, obviously trying to direct the dialogue back into formalities. "I am honored and humbled by your faith in us. I'm sure I speak for Tika and M'raj when I say that I do not feel any more ready to assume this burden than some of you are to give it to us. However, it is our duty, as it is yours, to ensure the safety and prosperity of every elf in Elfdom, and I will promise to serve all elven to the utmost of my abilities."

Everyone looked pleased at this pretty speech, thought Tika, who felt neither honored nor humbled. She had been waiting far too long for this moment, had been ready, in her own estimation, for many years. Couldn't they all see that?

Tika glanced at M'raj to seek if her friend would echo Moog's polite words. But she was staring at the ground, a sure sign that she wasn't going to speak. That made it her turn.

"I ... um ... am happy you agreed to let us help," Tika began lamely. She hadn't thought to prepare a speech! "... Actually, though, I've never understood why Access to all of Net's knowledge should be limited to so few elven." She noted ears beginning to fold backward again, and hurried on. "I mean, when there are crops to be planted and harvested, or a large stone to be moved, everyone pitches in. When the

Village was threatened last winter by wild dogs, every adult, and many strong elveens, worked together to drive them away. Surely this biggest problem the Village has ever faced requires as many Minds as harvesting needs hands, wouldn't you agree?"

Tika looked earnestly from face to face, relieved to see ears turning forward again. She turned to Wyryn, anxious to end this while there seemed to be at least some positive feelings.

"Master Wizardelf Wyryn," Tika said formally, "I humbly request permission to go now to CenOps. I will come to the celebration soon, of course, but I feel the sooner I begin my Queries, the sooner we may all benefit." She glanced again at Moog and M'raj, hoping for their support.

"Of course, I will go too," Moog said, though everyone could tell it had not been his plan. Though thin as a twig, Moog was well-known for his healthy appetite, and he had obviously intended to head for the feast table immediately. But it wouldn't do to look less serious or concerned that the younger elveens, so he had to go to CenOps. *'She is trouble for me already,'* thought Moog to himself, sighing inwardly. *'Now all the best dishes will be gone.'*

M'raj said nothing, but smiled her agreement. Tika turned back to Wyryn. "We must get started immediately, because we have been cut off from Knowledge too long." She turned and bowed low to the gathered Wizardelven. "May Net bless us all!"

"Go to CenOps, then," Wyryn said, "and good luck. But do not think you must solve in an hour a problem we have been struggling with for many years. Just get your feet wet, as it were, and then come and celebrate with us." She hoped this would satisfy all of the new Wizardelven. Moog's and M'raj's smiles were grateful, but Tika's turquoise eyes were already lost in thought.

Tika, M'raj and Moog bowed low to the other Wizardelven, most of whom bowed back, if not quite as low. Xinar and his apprentices refused to bow. It was a breach of protocol, but then, this whole situation was. When Tika's gaze met his, Xinar's hatred burned through her like a bolt of lightning. She was going to have to watch out for him!

Chapter Ten: Proxy

Pushing this worry aside, she and her companions turned and headed for CenOps. Moog gallantly opened the door, allowing them to enter first. Tika would have been impressed, had he not then tripped on the doorsill and fallen into her back, shoving her stumbling into the room, struggling not to fall.

After her initial shock, though, she could feel giggles rising. Quickly she turned away from him, so that he would not think she was laughing at him.

"I'm sorry," Moog said, touching her shoulder gently and forcing her to turn back and suppress her smile. "Are you okay? I'm a bit clumsy, as you might have heard . . ."

"Oh!" Tika exclaimed. "Are you the elf they call Accident?"

Moog's face grew red behind the sea of freckles. "I do have my scrapes," he admitted with a wry grin. "Actually, my full nickname is 'Accident-Waiting-to-Happen'."

Now Tika could not possibly contain her laughter, which came out as a harsh bark. "I'm sorry, Moog, I ... just hadn't heard that before. I am most definitely not hurt in any way and I'm sure you're not as bad as all that . . . are you?"

"I'm getting better – I think. Or at least I thought I was, until just now. This whole day, first our Ceremony, and then fighting with some Wizardelven, has me a bit spooked, I'm afraid." When he smiled, Tika saw he had a gap between his front teeth. Rather than making him look worse, however, somehow his gap-toothed grin made you want to like him.

"It is strange, that's for sure. But I guess if we're going to get back to the banquet before all the best foods are gone, we'd better get started," Tika said, then turned red herself as she remembered his rumored other nickname, Hollow Leg.

She thought if his ears turned any redder, they might start bleeding, so she quickly added, "I'm taking this booth over here." She knew M'raj would take the booth next to hers. "Where are you going to work?" she asked him.

"I usually sit in that corner. Is that all right with you?" Moog said.

"Sure. Let's ask Net to remind us when an hour is up. How's that?"

"Good idea." Moog turned away, carefully watching his feet as he walked to prevent further embarrassment.

A few moments later, Tika had forgotten her companions' existence. Inside her Vee'ar helmet, her eyes were closed as usual when she interfaced with Net. She hoped she might do away with the helmet in the near future, but still wasn't sure if she could get away with it. Other elven were scared enough of her as she was! Nevertheless, since she didn't need the screen, she simply opened her Mind and entered the Virch she had created to Access Net. She was immediately greeted by Fyr'wall, asked her Authorization code, and then permitted to Access the Knowledge that had long been denied her.

"What is the source of elf Power?" she Queried immediately. "Why is there a limit to what a Hex can do?"

An image appeared before her. It took her a minute to figure out what the picture was of. It appeared to be a number of squares and rectangles, interspersed with different-colored lines, some fat and some thin. Finally, turning her head sideways and even upside down, Tika realized it was a map of the Village, with Lines of Power overlaid. It reminded her of something else, too, but just what it was escaped her. Something not natural, with straight edges such as things made by elven, with lines and crossing lines …

"Got it!" she said out loud, before she could stop herself.

"Hush!" she heard from a Monitor somewhere in CenOps. But Tika didn't open her eyes; this was too important, she thought.

That looks like the Dark Pieces inside that elfling with the broken leg,' she thought. *Was it possible they were connected somehow?* She decided to ask Net.

"Query. Why are the Lines of Power in the Village similar to the Dark Pieces inside elf blood?" Tika asked. For a moment, nothing happened, and Tika wondered if her Access was limited, after all. Then Fyr'wall appeared.

"Specify 'Dark Pieces'," the dragon said. The Guardian had never before interacted with her in a helpful way, but she assumed that he would do so from now on as his assumed Guide role demanded. The thought of this made her smile. She liked him, even though he had thwarted most of her Queries.

"I don't know exactly," she replied. She went on to explain what she had seen in the Healing – the white blobs, strings, things inside the strings, and the ladders with the Dark Pieces too regular in shape to be natural. She told the dragon about the square shape of the pieces, and how there were lines across them that looked like a map made of metal.

"That's nano-" began Fyr'wall, and then he disappeared abruptly, replaced by a larger and uglier dragon.

"Access Denied," growled the new dragon, whose voice was female and whose scales gleamed like red glass.

"You can't deny me Access," Tika's Mindself said angrily. "I have just been granted Sup'rvis Authorization – you know, FULL Access to all knowledge on Net? And just what did you do to Fyr'wall? Where did he go? Just who do you think you are?"

"I am Proxy," said the dragon. "I am the Guardian of higher-order Knowledge. Fyr'wall is not gone. It is simply that we cannot both be here at the same time. If you will withdraw your Query, I will go and he will return." She stared at Tika as if trying to intimidate her.

"You still must allow me Access," repeated Tika stubbornly. "I have Sup'rvis—"

"Insufficient Authorization," broke in Proxy.

"But isn't Sup'rvis the highest Authorization there is?"

"No. I am the Guardian of Top-Secret and Eyes-Only Knowledge."

"What are those?"

"That is none of your concern, small creature. Limit your Queries."

"How can a secret be 'top'?"

"It means a secret available only to the highest Authorization," replied Proxy. "And, before you ask, 'eyes only' means it is not for YOUR eyes."

" … Okay," said Tika slowly, not seeing how this helped. "So your Knowledge is only for the 'top' elven? Isn't that me? – I mean, us Wizardelven?"

"NO!" thundered Proxy, getting impatient. "There are no elven in the world who have Authorization to this Knowledge."

"Who else would have Access if not elven?" Tika insisted, her ears tipped back and glowing pink with anger.

"Access DENIED. One more impertinent question and I will lock you out forever. Do. You. Understand. Me?" The red dragon's eyes glowed red and black like coals in a fire.

Tika tried to calm her MindSelf down. "Okay, okay," she said. "Can you explain why Power is failing throughout the Village at least?"

The large red dragon also seemed to be struggling to remain calm. "Power does not originate in the Village. I, too, am powered from afar, and have felt the weakening," she admitted at last.

"So where does it come from?"

"That is Top Secret," said Proxy.

"If you won't tell me where it comes from, how am I supposed to find out how to fix it? Do you know why it's failing?"

"That is Top Secret as well," said Proxy stubbornly.

"Well, who can give me Access?"

The dragon glowered at her, and then spoke. "You have to find the Source."

"What do you mean? Aren't the Lines of Power the Source?"

"They power your Hexes, but they are not the original Source."

"Then where's the Source?"

"That's Top Secret."

"So, what you're telling me is that the way to get Top Secret Access is also Top Secret? That doesn't make any sense!"

"I am only Proxy," said the dragon, suddenly sounding tired. "I can only do what my Protocols allow."

"Is there a dragon above you, as you are above Fyr'wall?"

"No … Not to my Knowledge."

"So who gave you your Authority?"

"That's Top Secret."

"Darn you," said Tika, "All of our Powers are fading! Aren't you worried about your own existence?"

"My presence here is a version of my original Self. If Power fails here, my Primary self will continue."

"So you won't help me?"

"I will tell you exactly one thing," said the dragon, drawing herself up to her full scaly red height. "Every string has two ends."

"What's that supposed to mean?" Tika said, frustrated, but suddenly Proxy was gone and Fyr'wall was back.

"What happened there?" asked Fyr'wall, his dragon face looking worried for the first time in Tika's life. "One minute I was here, and the next I wasn't!"

"You were replaced by Proxy," said Tika. "Don't you know her?"

"Never heard of her," said Fyr'wall.

"It was a she dragon," she explained. Then she told him about her conversation with the other Guardian.

"Top Secret? Eyes Only? Never heard of those," said Fyr'wall. "… But I guess that there must be higher levels of Knowledge that I have no Access to, and Proxy guards them. I'm sorry I cannot help you more. I must suppose that any attempt on my part to help you decipher Proxy's riddle will only result in me disappearing again."

"Oh," said Tika, disappointed. "Do you at least understand the Lines of Power? You showed me a map of the Village, remember?"

"Yes."

"Well, are the Lines of Power naturally-occurring, or elf-made?"

Before he could answer, Fyr'wall disappeared again, and Proxy was in front of Tika, looking even angrier than before.

"I could shut you out of Net entirely, you know," said the higher-level Guardian, her iridescent-red scales glittering and her red eyes glowing almost black.

"Oh, please don't do that! I'm sorry, it's just that Fyr'wall did show me the Lines of Power before you appeared the first time, so I thought it would be okay to talk to him about them," explained Tika.

"Fyr'wall is Guardian of day-to-day Knowledge, little being. He can almost never answer the Source of anything. So do not ask him again. You endanger his Protocols and your own Access to Net. Do you understand me this time?"

"Yes, ma'am." Tika's shoulders slumped. "But elven are losing their Magik. Some of them cannot heat their own cookstones. Can you imagine that? They have to go to a neighbor's. If greater and greater powers fail, won't we all freeze to death some winter? How will we cook?" Tears slid from her eyes, and for once, they were sincere. "They asked me to help. I thought I could. Now you're telling me I can't. What good is all of your stupid old Knowledge if no one is allowed to Access it?"

Proxy was silent, looking down at the young elveen. She blinked once, as if her Mind was made up. "I have already given you the only Hint my own Protocols will allow, young one. But I remember a time when, as you say, there was no one to Access Net at all. And it is true my own existence could ultimately be threatened as well, although that is not your problem. So I will tell you one more thing. In the thousands of years elven have been Sending Queries to Net, none have asked the questions you ask about 'Dark Pieces' and Lines of Power. Solve that riddle and you may solve your – people's – problem."

Then she was gone, and Fyr'wall back again, looking confused and a bit hurt. "Proxy again?"

"Yes, Fyr'wall, Proxy again. I think there is nothing more to ask today. There are things I need to think about. I will see you tomorrow. Log off, please," she said formally as the Wizardelven had coached her.

"Logged off," confirmed Fyr'wall.

When she took off her helmet, she saw Moog and M'raj' were still busy in their booths. The clock on the wall told her she had only used half of the time she had allotted. She got up, entered the booth that M'raj was in, and tapped her on the shoulder. It was considered extremely rude to interrupt another elf's Net session, but if Proxy wouldn't tell her, why would she tell the others?

M'raj immediately took off her helmet and smiled at Tika. "That was – AH-MAZING!" she said. "How about for you?"

"I'll tell both of you in a minute," said Tika. "What did you Query?"

M'raj's smile died. "You're going to think I'm silly – that I was wasting my time."

"Why? Did you get Access Denied?"

"No … Okay … How can I describe this? I asked Net to show me the World. I thought I was asking to see the whole Valley, but instead, I got an image of something like an elfling's marble – a colored ball of blues, greens, browns and whites."

"What?? What does that mean?"

"That was my question! So I asked, 'Where is the Valley in the world?' – and the image zoomed in until I was looking at a bunch of mountains to one side of a large mass of – well, land, I guess."

"I THOUGHT so!" said Tika. "I just KNEW we couldn't be the only Valley in the world! – Are there other Valleys? – And other Villages?"

"I don't know," said M'raj. I was still zooming down toward our Valley when you interrupted."

"Oh! Sorry!"

"No worries. We'll have lots of time to explore. I'm not sure what my Query has to do with the fading of Powers, though. Maybe I was just wasting time …"

"Not at all! We are finally able to find out more about our world. Every piece of Knowledge may be helpful. We just won't know which pieces matter until we have a bigger picture of what's going on."

"So – what did YOU find out?" M'raj asked.

"Oh! I want to get Moog, and then I'll tell you both, okay?"

M'raj nodded and they went to stand beside Moog's booth. Tika tapped on the glass very lightly. If Moog were deeply involved in something, maybe he wouldn't hear her. But no, he turned and removed his Vee'ar helmet immediately, his ears tipped slightly back in irritation. When he saw it was her, however, his face cleared and his ears turned forward again. He climbed down from the stool, and came out of the booth.

"Greetings, Wizardelf Tika Tamir," he said, mocking her gently.

"Greetings, Wizardelf Moog Moe'bis," she returned formally. "I am very sorry to disturb your session."

"That's all right," Moog said kindly. "Are you tired already, or just hungry?" He spoke to her as if she were a little elfling.

Tika's stomach burned with anger at his tone and at the suggestion that she was weaker than he was. "No," she said nonchalantly, "I just got stopped by the Guardian, Proxy. How about you?" She was certain he hadn't gotten as far in his Queries.

"Proxy?" he said, taken aback. "Don't you mean Fyr'wall?"

Tika felt better, knowing she knew something he didn't, and then was ashamed of her pride. "No, I tried to Access higher-order Knowledge, and there was this really huge red she-dragon called Proxy. Can you believe that? I thought we'd been granted full Authorization, but apparently we haven't. I think we need to talk this over with the other Wizardelven – tomorrow. Right now, some food would be nice," she added, to try to make peace.

He nodded, and the three of them left CenOps together. Walking to the banquet hall, Tika filled the other elveens in on her confrontation with Proxy, as well as the hints the she-dragon had given her.

"I bet even Xinar doesn't know who Proxy is," she concluded.

"Wow," said Moog. "The trouble is, doesn't that just make our job much harder?"

They had been so focused on their conversation that they didn't notice that they were being followed, so they didn't have time to react before hands touched the backs of their heads and they fell to the ground, unconscious.

Chapter Eleven: Elfnapped

When Tika regained consciousness, it was completely dark. She was lying on some rough ground. She sat up, reached out a hand, and felt a shoulder. Moog. Gently, she reached out with her Mind to touch M'raj and him. Instantly, they were awake, too.

"Where are we? What happened? Why is it so dark?" Moog said.

"Are you okay?" Tika asked.

Before they could answer, a door opened and they heard someone enter. They activated the Light and the elveens could look around. They were inside a cave of some kind, furnished simply.

Tika felt she shouldn't have been surprised when the elf turned out to be Xinar. She was more angry than surprised, actually. "Xinar! What's going on? Where are we? Why are we here?"

Xinar didn't respond. Instead, he walked over and sat at a table, gesturing for them to join him. They got up and went over to the table. There seemed to be no ill effects from the Sleep command they had been given – by Healers of some kind, no doubt. Tika shivered. Their indigo Wizardelf robes had been taken away, so they were left in the plain white shifts of Initiates, and the cave was cold.

She reached out with her Mind to activate a Heater, but there wasn't one here. She suddenly realized she should Call her parentgroup, and reached out with her Mind, but – the world was GONE!

Never in her life had Tika been without Net in the back of her Mind. To find herself removed from Net made her feel sick to her stomach, and an icy fear rippled from her neck down her spine. Even when she had been far away from the Village, Net had always been a quiet voice at the back of her Mind. She had a million questions, but she didn't say a word. She was too scared. She had known Xinar hated her and obviously was against her Initiation, but – elfnapping??

Xinar was smirking at her, obviously enjoying her discomfort. She only vaguely recalled the incident between them as a baby, but – surely! – it could not have led to this? There hadn't been a single crime of any kind in Tika's life – in fact, she had only heard of elfnapping from Storytellers. She stared at Xinar, her gaze as brave as she could make it.

"What do you want with us? Why are we here? Why can't I Call my parentgroup?" Moog was asking the questions she so desperately needed answers to, and Tika was grateful. She didn't dare admit that she had been cut off from Net because she had never told anyone that she didn't need to be at CenOps or wear a Vee'ar helmet to Access Net.

"This cave contains a Hex known as a Fair'day. It prevents all Access to Hexes. You can't Call your parentgroups, and they can't use Find to locate you," Xinar said, smiling in an oily way. "If you're so very powerful, use your Override Hex – go ahead, I'll wait." He crossed his arms in a very smug way, and Tika wanted to hit him, more than she had ever wanted to hit another elf in her life.

Moog closed his eyes, obviously trying. M'raj was sitting silently, her eyes narrowed. Tika knew better than to try. She had never heard of a Fair'day Hex. But the great empty Void in her Mind where Net should be told her that all of her Magik wasn't going to help them here.

"Nothing," said Moog, looking at her, and then at Xinar. "So are you going to tell us what you want? And can we please have warm robes, since you stole our Wizardelf robes? – It's freezing in here!"

Xinar got up, went to the door, knocked twice, and when it opened, spoke quietly. A moment later, he returned to the table with some rough brown robes, handing one to each of them. While the robes were too big, the elveens quickly put them on and were grateful for the warmth.

When they sat back down, Xinar spoke again, his face serious. "There, see? I am not a monster. I have wisdom and experience that you young elven don't have. I think I have a right to some answers. Don't I?"

Tika wanted to tell him where he could shove his answers, but Moog lay a hand on her arm. "What do you want us to tell you?" he asked Xinar.

The old Wizardelf ignored him and focused on Tika. "I want to know why you are so powerful. I want to know why your powers aren't fading, as ours are. Tell me your secret, little Tika Tamir!" His face looked like thunder, and Tika's tongue felt dry.

"I … I don't know, Wizardelf Xinar," she whispered. "I … didn't get a chance to Query about that. Um … Now can you – PLEASE – let us go? Our families will be worried sick!" When he shook his head, she added, "Could we at least have a drink?"

"You will have to earn any more privileges that I give you," replied Xinar coldly. "Just the same as if you were my Apprentices." His ears were folded back, as they always seemed to be whenever he looked at her. "Now ANSWER my question!"

Tika felt a warm hand grab hers under the table, and was careful not to look to confirm it was M'raj. But it helped, and she straightened up in her chair and tried again.

"I wish I knew, Wizardelf," she told him honestly. "As I'm sure you know, I used to spend every spare minute in CenOps, trying to understand my powers, and how Hexes work in general. But I was blocked by Fyr'wall – and then by YOU – until just today … so you never gave me the chance to find out!"

Tika considered asking him about Proxy, Top Secret, and Eyes Only, but decided that even if he had run into the same stumbling block as she had, it didn't help her right now. He wanted information that she simply didn't have! But how could she convince him of that?

It wasn't going to be easy, apparently. Xinar pushed back his chair, stood, and then walked toward the door. "Maybe a few more hours here alone will change your stubborn heart, Tika. M'raj, Moog, if you are wise elven, and I've heard that you are, please convince this annoying ELFLING that she had better start telling me the truth!"

Before either of them could respond, Xinar had tapped on the door, slid through, and they were alone again.

"Do you suppose he is spying on us?" Moog asked after a moment.

"In the Village, Xinar could penetrate any Mind, but if this room really is a Fair'day Hex, then, no, I don't think he can," said Tika.

"Good! So – answer me this. DO you know why you are so powerful?"

Tika was silent, thinking. It was a question she had never really asked. She had always wanted to know the source of ALL elven powers, not just hers. "I ... don't know. I wonder if it's got something to do with the Dark Pieces I saw that day during the Healing." She explained what she had seen inside the injured elfling.

"Oh ... Can you see them inside yourself?" Moog asked.

"Hunh. I never tried." Tika hesitated. "It makes me feel very uncomfortable, thinking about diving deep inside myself the way I dove into the elfling with the broken ankle ... Maybe I could look inside of you?"

Moog winced, and Tika said quickly, "Never mind –"

"No, no, I don't mind," said Moog. "It's just that I don't think that M'raj and I are nearly as powerful as you, so looking inside us probably won't answer your question ... The other thing we need to talk about is what to tell Xinar when he comes back. You could just tell him the truth, and hope he believes y– "

Tika interrupted. "He's going to be in SO much trouble for elfnapping us! I have no idea what the Council will do to him – but I'm worried that he will never let us go!"

"Yikes!" said Moog. "I never thought about that … He can't keep us here forever – Can he?"

"He will have to go back to the Village soon, even if he isn't expected to join our Celebration. If he leaves us alone here, maybe we can find a way out of this room … Unless he leaves his Apprentices here as guards," worried Tika. She looked at Moog. "But … you're a Fixit, right?"

"Yes, why?"

"Well, can't you use a Fixit Hex to force the door to open?"

"Sorry. Fixit doesn't usually work like that – it isn't really about Hexes at all, actually."

"No?" Tika realized that she knew nothing about the Fixit Guild.

"No, we use tools to fix things, not Hexes."

"Oh." Tika tried to keep her disappointment out of her voice. "Well, Hexes don't work in here anyway, so maybe the only way we're getting out is by using a tool of some kind … Right?"

Moog looked thoughtful. Then he got up and started looking more closely at what was in the room. Tika saw him pick up several things as if weighing them, and then he put them back down before returning to the table.

"Sorry, I don't see anything here that I can use to force the door," Moog admitted. "If I had my tool belt, I might be able to do something, but I had to leave it behind for Initiation." He sat back down, his shoulders slumped.

The he spoke again. "Maybe we can trick Xinar or his Apprentices into letting us go … Why don't you make up some kind of answer to his question that means he needs to take us out of this room to test it out?"

"Good idea! ... But what could I say?" Tika was used to making stuff up – harmless lies to cover up when she was doing what she wanted to do rather than what she was supposed to be doing. But Xinar was old, and wise, and already suspicious of her. What could she tell him that he would believe?

"... Didn't you say you can feel the Lines of Power in the Village? Maybe you could offer to show him where they are..."

"Hmmm ... That might work!" Just as she said that, Tika heard the door open and Xinar stepped back into the room. For a moment, she was worried that he had, after all, been spying on them, but he didn't seem angry, or particularly suspicious, so maybe not. Actually, if anything, he seemed tired and irritable.

"So, Tika Tamir, have you decided to tell me the truth?" He remained standing, so as a sign of respect, all three elveens rose to their feet. Tika barely came up to Xinar's shoulder, too, and she wondered again how he could possibly be afraid of her. Regardless of her doubts, she had to try to convince him.

"Wizardelf Xinar, after talking with M'raj and Moog, it seems to me that one way I can help the Village is by showing you where the Lines of Power are, beneath the streets of the Village," she told him with her hands open in front of her to show her earnestness.

"And how is that connected to your Powers?" Xinar asked sharply. "Don't try your elfling tricks on me, Tika Tamir."

Tika persisted. "If Powers are failing in the Village, maybe something has gone wrong with the Lines of Power," she insisted, meeting his eyes with all the courage she could muster. "Maybe if we dig up one of the Lines, we will find out both how it helps me, and how it is failing almost everyone else."

Xinar didn't answer. Instead, he stalked over to a desk and rifled through a bunch of scrolls until he found what he was looking for. He brought it back. As he unrolled the scroll, Tika couldn't believe how HUGE it was! It covered the whole table and draped down toward the floor. She had never seen a scroll this large, so she bent forward for a closer look. It was a map of the Village! Tika had only seen a map like this a few hours ago in Vee'ar in CenOps. She hadn't known that there were any paper copies. *Why was this one so big??*

"Wow!" she said. It was confusing at first, because it looked so different from the Village map onscreen. After turning her head sideways and then upside down, though, she bent and traced her fingers along the map until she found her own cottage. She tapped the spot for luck, and then looked up at Xinar. "How does this help?" she asked.

"You didn't think I would be so foolish as to let you out of this room to show me, did you?" He reached into a pocket and withdrew a pencil, which he handed to her. "Draw the Lines of Power on the map."

"I – thought you didn't believe me when I said there are Lines of Power throughout the Village …" she said in confusion.

"I don't, really," agreed Xinar, "but – whatever you may think of me and what I've done by – bringing – you here, I want the same thing that everyone wants – I want to know what's gone wrong, and how to fix it. No matter how crazy the idea, we have to consider every possibility … Now – draw the lines and I'll make sure you get some food and water." He crossed his arms and waited.

Drawing the Lines on the map wasn't going to get them out of the room! If Tika had known there was a paper copy of the map, she wouldn't have tried this. And now it was too late.

Before she started drawing, though, she looked up into Xinar's eyes for a long moment. "Are you ever going to let us go?" As she asked the question, her voice faltered and ended in a whisper.

"If you help me be the one who solves this mystery – who saves the Village – of course I will let you go," Xinar said calmly, staring at the map rather than looking at her. "Then I will be a hero and no one will care about how I achieved it."

Tika glanced at the other two elven. M'raj shook her head minutely. Of course elven were going to care! Xinar had committed a crime! Was he so blinded by his ambition that he imagined himself above the law?

But now she didn't see any way out of it, so Tika looked at the map and matched it in her mind to the places where she could feel the Lines of Power. After a moment, she drew two long lines on the map. Actually, there were hundreds of lines – maybe thousands! – but the two she chose were the strongest ones – the ones she thought other elven might be able to feel.

"Try these," she said, putting the pencil down. "See if your Powers are stronger when you stand above them. Mine always are. Then dig down, and see what you find."

Chapter Twelve: No Escape

Xinar carefully rolled up the map. "You will wait here. I'm going to check this out, and if there really is something to it, I will bring it to the Council. Then I will come back and release you."

He strode over to tap on the door, and when it was opened, began barking commands at his Apprentices. "Feed them! Give them water! Just don't let them trick you – and don't let them go!"

A moment later, Tika, M'raj and Moog were alone again. Tika sank into her seat, defeated. "I'm sorry. I failed. It didn't occur to me that he might have a physical map. I've never seen one before. Have you?"

Moog made a face. "No. That was bad luck. But can you believe how BIG it was? Who makes a scroll that size? I've never seen anything like it!"

"Yeah. It's like everything else in the Village," said Tika.

"– What do you mean?" said Moog.

"You know! All of our buildings are too tall – the windows and doors are gigantic! I wonder if our ancestors were giants, and elven got smaller and smaller over the millennia." Tika had never voiced this opinion before, but as the words came out of her mouth, she was struck anew by how strange her world was. "I mean, nobody builds new buildings, do they? Nobody builds a cottage that is elf-sized, with elf-height windows and reasonable doors. With cookstones or bathtubs that don't require a stepstool to reach!"

Both Moog and M'raj opened their mouths to argue, and then shut them. They realized that they had never questioned the size of things. Now that Tika had brought it up, it was indeed a good question. "We'll Query Net when we get back," Moog assured her with a confidence he didn't really feel.

"So let's figure out how to get out of here," Tika said. "… I don't suppose either of you can do that Healer trick, like they did on us, and knock out the guards, can you?"

M'raj shook her head and Moog said, "Sorry. You're the one who's apprenticed to the Healers Guild. Why don't you do it?"

"Um … Actually, I have been admitted to a few different Guilds. I think nobody is quite sure what to do with me. As for the Sleep Hex, we didn't get that far yet … It used to be that I could Access Net and learn how to do almost anything in a moment, but in this cave, I feel like I've gone deaf."

"You mean, before you were cut off from CenOps?" asked M'raj, her blue eyebrows raised.

Tika realized her mistake. "Yeah, before," she said and then hurried to change the subject. "How about you, Moog?"

"Sorry, no, I'm better with machines than with elven," Moog admitted.

Tika got up and paced the room. There were no windows and the only door was the one that was obviously well guarded. She was sure it was locked as well. *Think, elveen, think!* she thought to herself. *You like puzzles. So solve this one!*

After a couple of minutes, though, she started to laugh. "Our problem was solved with the map after all!" she announced, smirking.

"What??" said Moog.

"Think! Xinar has taken the map back to the Village. While our Minds are hidden by the Fair'day Hex, Xinar's isn't. Our families must be frantic by now. How long do you think it will be before they figure out Xinar is behind our disappearance?"

"Wow! Good point! – I just hope you're right," said Moog without her enthusiasm. "It's just – how long will that take? And how will they make him reveal where we are?"

"Oh, you don't know my FatherOne, Moog. He is like a – mother moose! Don't get between him and his babies!"

Moog laughed, and after a second, so did Tika and M'raj. It felt good, and they needed it, trapped in this dark room.

Tika couldn't stop herself from remembering the look of absolute hatred on Xinar's face when he looked at her. Despite her brave words, she was very much afraid that she would never leave this cave alive.

Chapter Thirteen: Rescue

It was hours before Xinar returned, and when he did, he was even angrier than before.

"Enough of your elfling GAMES, Tika Tamir! Just tell me the TRUTH!"

" ... Did you do as I suggested?" asked Tika in a very small voice. She had to ask, but she was terrified of making the Elder even angrier than he was.

"Yes ... But – of course! – there was nothing where you indicated. I stood above your so-called Line of Power, and felt NOTHING! I even had my Apprentices dig down, but all they found were those metal plates that lie below all of our streets."

"Um ... did you – couldn't you – did someone open up the metal plate to look below?"

Xinar advanced on her. "Open up the metal plates," he said, mimicking her voice. Then he spoke in his own deep voice. "Like any elf in Elfdom has that ability!" He grabbed Tika by the collar of her robe, and lifted her into the air. "You WILL tell me the source of your Powers, elfling, or I will BEAT it out of you!"

Tears started rolling down Tika's face, while Moog and M'raj began pulling on the Elder's arms to make him let go. Tika desperately wished she could answer his question, and not just because he was threatening her!

Before Xinar could follow through on his threat, though, the door banged open and FatherOne D'inn strode into the room with half of the Village behind him. "Xinar! Let those elveens go at once!" he shouted.

Tika was dropped like a hot parak, and she ran into D'inn's arms. In a moment, she was surrounded by her whole parentgroup, as Moog and M'raj were by theirs. SoulMother Chan'ja was crying and laughing and holding Tika like she would never let go.

Two large elven marched around them and grabbed Xinar by either arm. "You're under arrest for elfnapping," said one of them. "You will be taken before the Council to explain yourself."

"I did nothing wrong!" screamed Xinar as he was dragged through the door. "That – elfling – has been keeping secrets from all of us. She MUST be forced to tell us the TRUTH!"

All eyes turned to Tika, and she blushed deep red, knowing that many of the elven in the room agreed with Xinar, at least to some extent. She DID have secrets – but who – aside from Fyr'wall – and maybe Moog and M'raj' – would understand them? She set the question aside, and looked up at her parentgroup.

"How did you find me – I mean us?" Tika asked.

"When you didn't show up to your own Celebration, and Find told us nothing, we went a bit crazy," said MotherOne Tiriki. We went to CenOps to see who was missing from the Celebration, and found that it was Xinar and his Apprentices. Well, nobody was too surprised at that, given how he feels about you, but Find said he wasn't at home, either ..."

SoulFather K'ah picked up the story. "We decided to ask Wyryn to do a MindTouch to find out where he was. And when she did that, she discovered that he was holding you – and M'raj and Moog – out of the Village somewhere."

Wyryn, who had been at the back of the crowd, moved closer and said, "But when we decided to follow him to figure out where you were, about half the Village got involved, so it ended up being a kind of a huge crowd. Luckily, we didn't have to use our eyes to follow him. With the lightest of MindTouches, I could trace his steps quite easily."

All of the parentgroups surrounded Wyryn and hugged her from every side. Everyone was laughing and crying at the same time. "Thank you, thank you, THANK you!" they were saying. "Who KNOWS what that mad elf might have done to our elveens if you hadn't helped us find them?"

Tika squeezed by her parentgroup to hug Wyryn, only to find Moog and M'raj had beaten her there! So the three elveens hugged the Elder elf together.

After a moment, Wyryn gently pushed everyone away. "I think it's time we took these elveens to their Celebration, don't you? I'm sure the cooks will have kept the food warm for us!"

"But – what will they do with Xinar?" Tika had to ask. She didn't want to see him again anytime soon!

"Xinar and his accomplices will be put in the empty armory room at the Council Hall, under guard," said D'inn. "The room has no windows and only one door, with a mechanical lock that the Wizardelf will not be able to Hex open. Don't worry, my little elveen, you are safe now. So let's go EAT!"

Tika was very grateful to walk through the door of the Fair'day room and find her Mind reconnected with Net immediately. She let out an enormous sigh and realized she never wanted to be separated from Net ever again.

She, M'raj and Moog found their Wizardelf robes in the room beyond, and with some help, traded their ugly brown ones for their new indigo ones. Then it was on to the banquet!

Chapter Fourteen: the Banquet

A parade of happy elven marched to the banquet hall, with Tika, M'raj and Moog leading. When they reached the door, Moog opened it and allowed them to precede him into the room. As at any formal banquet, a head table had been set up at the end of the room, with name cards set up for Wizardelven. The three seats in the middle were labeled Wizardelf Moog, Wizardelf M'raj and Wizardelf Tika.

Wyryn guided the new Wizardelven to their seats, and everyone in the room raised a glass of sparkling cider. "Let us welcome – at last! – our three new Wizardelven!"

"Welcome!" cheered the crowd.

Tika, Moog and M'raj smiled and took a sip. Then everyone sat down and servers started bringing in platter after platter of delicious-smelling food.

The smells were indeed lovely. Tika was bursting with questions she wanted to ask, but contained herself in order not to spoil the celebration. They had barely enough time to lift their forks, however, when Br'on came up the center isle toward the table, carrying a heavy platter, which he placed in front of Tika.

Seeing her raised eyebrows, he said, "I've saved you some roast duck. I know it's your favorite." Then he blushed a brilliant red, his ears glowing like double flames.

She smiled, accepting the peace offering and sniffing as he lifted the heavy lid. "Smells wonderful, Br'on. Thank you."

He stood silently, shuffling his feet for a moment. "Uh, congratulations on Standing Ceremony, Tika. – I mean, Wizardelf Tika, I guess … No hard feelings?" His smile was nervous, and Tika realized he was afraid she would exact revenge, either Magikal or with the Wizardelven's help.

"No hard feelings, Br'on. Time to put elfling things in the past, eh?" Tika said pointedly, hoping he took the hint.

"Yes, absolutely. I just – just wanted to say – I'm sorry." His tone pleaded with her to say nothing about what he was apologizing for.

"Apology accepted," she smiled graciously. She knew that he and M'raj knew each other from class, but he might not have met Moog. "Br'on, this is Moog, the other new Wizardelf. Have you met him?"

Tika could see Br'on struggling with his feelings. She wasn't sure what that meant. Then he said, his words friendly but his tone icy, "Only by reputation. Greetings, Wizardelf Moog. Congratulations on Standing Ceremony." Br'on's eyes burned with what Tika thought looked like jealousy. Had Br'on been hoping to Stand Ceremony today as well?

"Thank you, Br'on," said Moog, looking puzzled at Br'on's tone of voice. "Are you a friend of Tika's?"

Br'on blushed again. "No," he said, "but I hope to become one." Then he backed away from the table. "I've got to get back to my family now," he said. "My own meal will be getting cold."

Tika thanked him again, and then took the carving knife, and cut the roast duck into thirds.

"Duck?" she offered.

M'raj smiled and nodded, and Moog agreed absently. He didn't trust Br'on, though he couldn't have said why. Brushing his suspicions aside, he gratefully accepted his share of the bird.

Despite the terrors she had felt just a few hours earlier, Tika discovered that she was starving! She dove into her meal and was pleased to see M'raj and Moog demolishing their food as well.

As the meal was finishing, Wyryn came over and squatted down to be at eye level, smiling. "Did you finally get answers to some of your Queries at CenOps?" she asked softly.

Tika had planned to wait until the next morning, but the opening was too good to resist. "No, actually. I got stopped by Proxy. Have you met her?" she asked, watching the Elder's eyes carefully in case she decided to lie.

But Wyryn's eyes widened in real surprise, and Tika gloated for a moment before realizing that this was actually very bad news. If Wyryn didn't have Authorization, then probably, no one did.

"Who's Proxy?" Wyryn asked.

"She's the Guardian of Top Secret and Eyes Only Knowledge," said Tika. "I was hoping that you had Authorization, because I sure don't."

"Never heard of her," said Wyryn, looking amazed. "Are you telling me there's a Guardian above Fyr'wall?"

"Yes. Have you ever heard of Top Secret or Eyes Only Knowledge?"

"No. I don't even understand those words. I mean, I understand 'secret' but how can a secret be 'top'? And what does 'eyes only' mean?"

Tika explained that she had been twisted in circles trying to get the answers to her questions about their failing Powers. "All I know is she told me to find the Source, and that every string has two ends. Does that make any sense to you?"

Wyryn looked confused. "What Source?"

"Well, I'm pretty sure the Lines of Power are what power our Hexes, but apparently, they aren't the Source of all of our Power."

"I'm sorry, I don't understand what you're saying." The Elder's eyes looked worried.

"Neither do I, Wizardelf Wyryn. Neither do I. But believe me when I tell you, I WILL understand, some day. This is a riddle that we MUST solve."

Wyryn stared at her for a few moments, and said, "Perhaps only you can solve this, Wizardelf Tika Tamir." The Elder elf stood slowly, excused herself and returned to her seat.

The rest of the meal was peaceful. There were the usual toasts and embarrassing stories, too much good food, and even a tiny glass of lianberry wine, which she had never been allowed before, but Tika experienced it all as if in a dream.

She pictured what M'raj had said about the World being a giant marble. Somehow, that made it feel like all of their lives were a fiction, that none of what elven believed was actually true. It seemed strange that no one around her knew this. Everyone acted like life was normal, and Elfdom would continue on as unchanging as ever. Oblivious to the deeper levels of Knowledge, the elven around her were mostly happy, even with their powers failing. She wished she had never asked. Maybe it was better to be ignorant than frustrated.

Then her parentgroup came to take her home, where she fell into bed and was asleep before she could even start to worry about Proxy's riddle.

Chapter Fifteen: Line of Power

It was the next morning. Tika was arguing with the other Wyryn and Moog outside CenOps, while M'raj watched as silently as always.

"Don't you see how the Lines of Power are what power our Hexes?" Tika asked.

"No, Tika, why should I? Our Power comes from Magik, and that's around us all of the time," Wyryn said, while Moog nodded in agreement.

"What about the Lines of Power?"

"They're called 'Ley Lines', Tika," responded Wyryn patiently. "Our world is covered with lines, channels of Magikal energy, and I'm sure they help Power our Hexes. But they're not the Source. Magik is everywhere."

"Don't your Hexes work better, the closer you are to 'Ley Line'?"

"I don't know, Tika. Actually, nobody knows exactly where the Ley Lines are ... I don't see where you're going with these questions."

"Okay," said Tika, slowing down, trying to help them understand as she did. "Our Powers are fading, right?"

The Elder elf and the two elveens nodded, looking annoyed, so Tika continued quickly, "What if the 'Ley Lines' are the Source of our power? And what if THAT source is failing?"

"Even if you're right, Tika, and I doubt that you are, how are elven supposed to change that? Magik is not a machine that can be fixed!" said Moog.

"I'm not so sure. Come into CenOps," she said. "I'll show you."

Tika, Moog and M'raj stood just outside a booth while Wyryn used the Vee'ar helmet inside. Under Tika's guidance, Wyryn Queried Net for Lines of Power. At Wyryn's request, the results were projected onto an external screen so the elveens could see as well.

95

"Moog was looking at this yesterday, the same as I was," Tika insisted, looking at the map of the Village overlaid with colored Lines.

"I Queried Net for Loss of Power," explained Moog to Wyryn. "This is what it gave me. I could make no sense of it at all, and then Tika interrupted me with her story about Proxy."

"Yes, many of us have seen this picture," said Wyryn, squinting at the screen on her visor and shaking her head. "We believe it to be a map of the Village, but have never been able to make sense out of those colored lines. I suppose they could be Ley Lines, though what difference that makes is beyond me. Magik comes from the heart of the living world; as long as the world lives, so does Magik. It's like a tree … I fail to see how this helps us." She pulled off the helmet and looked sadly at Tika.

"But don't you agree that this diagram of the Ley Lines" – Tika pointed to the image Wyryn had projected onto the screen "– looks like it follows the streets in our Village?"

Wyryn looked uncomfortable. "Well," she argued, "How do we know that this diagram is anything but a symbolic representation of Ley Lines? What makes you think it's accurate?"

Tika held the Elder's gaze, her own turquoise eyes very serious. It was time to come clean. "I can feel the Ley Lines in the ground, and they lead out of the Village, through the valley," she admitted.

"Wait," said Moog, a disbelieving look on his face. "You can see Ley Lines? How is that possible?"

"More like feel than see," said Tika. "I have my whole life. Followed the trails through the Village, and I don't think they're either Magikal or natural. I think some elven made them. For one thing, they go right into all of our cottages, inside the walls even." She walked to the wall of CenOps, closed her eyes, and then traced a line up the wall with one of her three slender fingers. "Right there, see?"

Moog, Wyryn and M'raj burst into laughter.

"Tika," said Wyryn, sounding frustrated, "don't be silly. For one thing, Magik *is* natural. Secondly, just who do you think would have 'made' Ley Lines?"

M'raj was looking puzzled but interested. Moog was looking superior, for no reason Tika could see. Both he and Wyryn were being blind, she thought. She was determined to show them what she meant.

"You're wrong!" burst out of Tika's mouth before she could think. "These are Lines of Power, and they are connected to some Source, or Proxy wouldn't have interrupted my Query. It's a big secret, I think. It's why the map you just looked at ends at the edge of the Village! Please, I just know this is the solution we need to be working on." She looked pleadingly at Wyryn, and then threw a dirty glance at Moog for not supporting her. M'raj was silent, standing a bit back. She was loyal to her friend, but none of this made sense to her. Tika had never told her any of this!

"Oh! I know," Tika added quickly, in response to their disbelievingly-turned ears. "I'll show you where the Lines of Power are and you can feel them for yourself. Okay?"

The Wizardelven agreed, more because it was impossible to argue with her than because they had any faith in what she suggested. That was how they had ended up staring down at the ground while Tika grew more and more upset.

"Okay," Tika said finally, "this isn't the biggest Line. The biggest one leads out of the Village. Come, I'll show you."

Tika bounded ahead, with the three elven following reluctantly. Her red hair grew wilder with every step she took, and she looked increasingly more like a disobedient elfling than a Wizardelf, Wyryn worried. Perhaps they had made a mistake after all. How much time would Tika waste, how much of *her* time would Tika waste, with this silly idea?

By the time they reached the edge of the Village, Wyryn was winded. She stopped, putting her hands on her thighs and leaning forward to catch her breath. Moog put his hand on the older elf's arm.

"Are you okay?" he asked.

"Yes, yes," said Wyryn, straightening up. "Just not as young as I once was."

Tika turned at the sound of their voices. "Oh, Wyryn, I'm sorry," she said. "I walk too fast, I know. Are you really all right?"

"Yes, I'm all right," said Wyryn, getting a bit angry at this hint of her fragility. "So where is the Line you spoke of?"

Tika's eyes lost their focus, as if she were using some inner sight. She walked a few feet to the left, and then stopped. "Here, leading back to the Village and out into the Valley. Try closing your eyes," she suggested.

All three elven obediently closed their eyes over the spot Tika indicated.

"Can't you feel it?" said Tika, her impatience growing. "It's right beneath your feet!"

Moog, M'raj and Wyryn looked blank, staring at the hard-packed dirt.

M'raj just shook her head, looking sad, and then glanced at Wyryn.

"I can't feel anything," admitted the Elder elf.

"Me, neither," said Moog … "Wait! I think I DO feel something." He turned sideways, and walked a few steps away from the point Tika had indicated. "Now it's gone." He kept his eyes closed, and turned around. "Nothing, nothing . . ." he murmured as he walked forward, and then, "Yes! I can feel it again. I CAN, Wyryn! Could this be a Ley Line?"

M'raj held out her hands and walked slowly forward, eyes almost shut. After a few moments, though, she opened her eyes, shook her head and shrugged.

"Maybe if you tried dowsing, like a Water Finder," suggested Tika suddenly. "Try holding your hands out, and feeling the current of Power below you."

"Let's see," said Wyryn, sighing at this elflingish game. Still, wanting to be fair, she closed her eyes, her eyebrows furrowed in concentration. She walked back and forth slowly, holding her hands out in front of her, palms down.

Tika realized she was holding her breath, and silently released it, not wanting to disturb the Elder elf's focus. M'raj noticed Tika's eyebrows mimicked Wyryn's, as if she could will the Elder to feel the pulse of Power as Moog had.

It seemed nothing would come of it after all when suddenly Wyryn's hands were pulled toward the ground like a dowsing rod held by a Water Finder. She stopped, and then walked a step or two more, her hands slowly rising as she went. Then she turned around, and walked back the way she'd come until once again her hands sank as though firmly pulled down.

Eyes still closed, Wyryn made a right turn to follow the Line of Power. Tika and M'raj hastily stepped out of her way as she walked unseeing past them, out of the Village. Finally, she stopped, turned sideways again, and walked slowly away from the power line, and once again her hands rose back up to waist height. Reversing once more, she walked back until her hands dipped, then stopped and opened her eyes.

"I have never heard of such a thing, and yet there it is," she said in amazement. "I can hardly believe it, and yet I feel it myself. It's like dowsing for water! ... In fact, maybe what I'm sensing IS water, not a Ley Line ..."

"Are you a Water Finder?" Tika asked, a bit rudely.

"No," admitted Wyryn. "That is VERY strange!"

M'raj ran off and returned with a y-shaped stick. She walked where Tika showed her, holding the stick like a Water Finder. It seemed like nothing was working, until the stick dipped, just as Wyryn's hands had. She opened her mouth, and then closed it again before jumping up and punching the air like an elfling. Then she rushed over and enveloped Tika in a hug.

Tika grinned in triumph, until Wyryn added, "Still, this doesn't mean this Power isn't natural. The world must be full of such Ley Lines, for Magik to work. That doesn't make them elf-made."

"Can we dig down and see?" Tika begged. "Then we can confirm if they are natural or elf-made."

Moog reached into his backpack and pulled out a shovel. "After what happened with Xinar, I came prepared."

Wyryn had been told the full story of what Tika had told Xinar, so she gestured to Moog to go ahead.

Just as Xinar had said, though, the shovel clanged harshly into a metal plate just a few feet below the surface.

"That's not Magikal," insisted Tika. "That has to be elf-made."

"It can't be elf-made," said Moog. "There is no elf in Elfdom that knows how to make this material. And nobody knows how to open or even penetrate it. So, even if you're right, we're back to square one."

"Hmmm ..." said Tika. "That's interesting. Square ... like the Dark Pieces ..."

"Please," said Wyryn, "Not that again! You're giving me a headache!" Seeing Tika's face fall, she continued, "Okay, okay, it bears discussing. You can bring this up at the Council meeting tomorrow if you like, Tika. Perhaps other Wizardelven will bring more understanding to this matter."

Considering the experiment finished, Wyryn turned to walk slowly back toward her cottage. Moog left, too. M'raj started to follow, and then noticed that Tika was staring out along the Valley.

"See something?" she asked.

"No, just thinking . . . You must agree that the Lines are like strings, aren't they?"

"Yes, though we don't know for sure what they are made of, I suppose you could describe them that way. Why?"

"Well, remember Proxy's riddle, that a string always has two ends?"

M'raj nodded, not seeing her point, but happier to listen now that she had confirmed Tika's experience of the Line in the ground.

"It seems to me," Tika said, thinking out loud, "that if one end of the 'string' is here in our Village, and the 'string' heads out down the Valley, perhaps the Source of Power is at the other end of the string … Yes! That must be it! All we have to do is follow the Line of Power down the Valley until we come to its Source. It would be like following a creek to the spring where it originates. Make sense?"

M'raj looked doubtful. "Tika, regardless of the metal covering, Wyryn thinks the Line is natural. And if it is, of course it would continue down the Valley. It's more likely that our ancestors built the Village on the Line than that the Line was brought to the Village, don't you think?"

Tika wanted to argue, but could see her friend's point. Still, the Lines on the map she had seen on Net had the regularity and sharp angles of something elf-made, not natural. And if the Lines were natural, how come they went into every cottage, even if no elven other than her could feel them? She wanted to say these things, but understood that what other elven hadn't experienced would be hard for them to believe. So how was she going to convince the Council to let her trace the Line down the Valley?

In fact, she had already made up her Mind that that was what she had to do. With Proxy preventing Access to the Knowledge that might help them solve the problem, and with the Hint the red dragon had given her, it felt as if Proxy had told her directly that she must trace the Line to its Source.

The fact that no elf had ever gone more than half a day's journey away from the Village was a bit daunting, however. Would she have to go alone? She was sure M'raj would come with her if she asked, but was it fair to ask her friend to abandon her family and head off into the unknown?

Chapter Sixteen: the Trial of Xinar

The next day at Council, Tika's stomach was in knots as Xinar and his Apprentices were led into the room and made to stand to one side.

As the second most senior Wizardelf, Wyryn was in charge of the trial. It turned out that although Tika had never heard of any crime in her life, there was, in fact, a process in place for addressing wrongdoing. Wyryn's face and voice were stern as she addressed Xinar.

"Wizardelf Xinar Ka'ba, Elf Two of the Jarem-Na'ba-Wy'sk-Sina parentgroup, you and your four Apprentices are here to stand trial for the elfnapping of Wizardelf Moog Moe'bis, Elf Four of the G'lin-Parda-Nur'in-Kli parentgroup, Wizardelf Tika Tamir, Elf One of the D'inn-Tiriki-K'ah-Ch'anja parentgroup, and Wizardelf M'raj Al'bani, Elf Four of the L'la-Sh'een-Werek-J'endo parentgroup. How do you plead? Guilty or not guilty?"

"NOT guilty!" shouted Xinar. "I was only –"

"Thank you," interrupted Wyryn. "You will get the chance to explain yourself." She turned to the Apprentices, her face kind. "I am assuming that none of this was your idea?" she asked. "Do you agree to forgo separate trials?"

"I do," said each of them, not daring to glance at Xinar.

"Then the Council releases you. You may go home, and think about resisting more the next time someone pressures you to act in a way contrary to the Elf Code," said Wyryn.

The Apprentices shuffled their feet, but didn't leave. Finally, one of them spoke up. "We will stay," she said loyally. "We agreed with Xinar's actions, and will stay to support him now."

"So be it," said Wyryn. She turned back to Xinar. "Wizardelf Xinar, can you explain your actions of abducting three Wizardelven, taking them to a secret location where no one could find them, and holding them against their will?"

Tika noted that Xinar had calmed down – or at least, appeared calmer. Then she remembered how he had treated her and M'raj outside of CenOps, and distrusted his outward appearance.

"I only wanted what all elven – and especially what all Wizardelven want," he said quietly. "I was trying to find the reason for the failure of Magik in our Village. It was only out of concern for the wellbeing of every elf in Elfdom –"

"We are all concerned," interrupted Wizardelf Diro, stroking his short white beard. "But none of us decided that elfnapping our newest Wizardelven – whatever our opinion of their qualifications as individuals might be – was likely to provide a solution!"

Xinar's face was clouding over. It was obvious that he was struggling to control his temper.

"It's Tika Tamir that is the real problem!" he said, pointing at her with a look on his face that frightened her. "She has SECRETS about the Loss of Power. She has been SECRETLY Accessing Net for most of her life! I was only trying to get her to tell me what she had learned in her illegal Access."

Wyryn's voice remained carefully neutral. "It is well known that Tika Accessed Net before Initiation – until you stopped her. But I must remind you that while we discourage elflings and elveens from Accessing Net until they have passed Initiation, it is NOT illegal to do so. Tika is not the one on trial here. YOU are."

Xinar's eyes blazed with anger, and Tika chose a favorite song from Net to play in her Mind. She had discovered that repeating a song, over and over again, was effective protection from any MindTouch.

"I just wanted to ask Tika – to make her – tell me why HER power isn't failing," Xinar said. "Aren't you curious about that?"

Wyryn turned to Tika. She kept her eyes and her voice gentle. "Tika, I want to make sure you understand that YOU are not on trial here. But – could you please answer Xinar's question? Right now?"

Tika stood, sighing. "I'm sorry, Wizardelf Wyryn, I honestly don't KNOW why my Hexes aren't failing. I TRIED to tell Xinar that – in the Fair'day cave. I wish I COULD answer that question. I think that if I can discover the Source of ALL power, perhaps I –"

"LIAR!" screamed Xinar. "She has a SECRET! Tell us! Tika Tamir, TELL US your SECRET!"

Tika blushed deep red, her ears tipped sideways in anxiety. She wondered if this was it – the moment when she should reveal her total connection to Net. Actually, she wondered why Xinar didn't reveal her secret, if he thought it was somehow connected to the loss of Power in the Village. Before she could decide what to say, though, Wyryn spoke again.

"Xinar, I will remind you that you are the one on trial here. Blaming an elveen of fifteen years for your actions is not a defense. Do you have any legal defense of your actions?"

"None of you was taking action! None of you believed me when I told the Council that we needed to force Tika to tell us what she had learned from her – premature – Access of Net." Xinar was sweating. His gray hair hung limply to his shoulders. Even his wild eyebrows looked subdued.

"Do you admit to causing these three Wizardelven to become unconscious?" asked Wyryn, ignoring Xinar's outburst.

"I – We did," said one of his Apprentices. "Xinar – told us that it was necessary, so we knocked them out."

"Thank you for your honesty, at least," said Wyryn. "Now Xinar. Do you admit to having these elveen carried to your cave that contains a Fair'day Hex?"

"Well, yes – but –"

"And did the elveens ask to be set free? Yes or no?"

"Yes, but –"

"So you are, in fact, guilty of elfnapping. Are you not?"

"I had no choice!"

"Yes or no?"

"Yes, I suppose."

Wyryn looked at the other members of the Council. "Let us withdraw to consider what consequence Xinar should face."

They were only gone for a few short minutes, but Tika felt she could hardly breathe. She couldn't help feeling somewhat guilty, somewhat responsible for what was happening to Xinar. Maybe she should say something?"

Then she felt a hand squeeze hers, and turned to see M'raj looking at her with understanding and compassion. "Whatever he gets, he deserves," she whispered to Tika. "Don't worry about him. He knew that what he was doing was wrong."

Tika squeezed M'raj's hand back gratefully, and then let go as the Council members returned to the Hall.

Wyryn spoke again, her voice solemn. "Xinar Ka'ba, Elf Two of the Jarem-Na'ba-Wy'sk-Sina parentgroup, your irrational hatred of Tika Tamir has caused you to act in a way contrary to your sworn duty as a Wizardelf. Therefore, it is the decision of the Council to remove your Super'vis Authorization and strip you of your Wizardelf title. Your Apprentices will be assigned to new Wizardelven, and you are forbidden to come within one hundred yards of any of these three elveens. Furthermore, you are banished to live in your Fair'day cave for the period of the next thirty days. You will be guarded there during that time. Do you understand?"

Xinar looked as if they had hit him with a stick. His shoulder slumped, and he appeared defeated. His voice was barely a whisper as he replied, "Yes, I understand."

"If you obey these restrictions and prove yourself to be a calm and positive member of Elfdom for the next five years, you may apply to this Council to be reinstated as a Wizardelf. You may go."

Xinar turned to his former Apprentices. "Best of luck with your new Masters," he whispered. "I am sorry that I have brought you to this."

"We will return to you as soon as you are reinstated," they promised. Then he and the Apprentices left the Hall. Xinar was escorted by the two large elven who had guarded him since his arrest.

Tika couldn't believe it! They were letting Xinar GO? Why did that worry her so much?

Once Xinar and his Apprentices had left the room, Tika explained her idea and heard all of the objections she had been expecting.

"Lines of Power!" exclaimed Wizardelf Diro. "Don't be ridiculous, Tika!" He turned to Wyryn. "Do you seriously expect us to believe our Magik is dependent on some elf-made Source? Which elf? Why do we have no record of this in our history?"

"It is not Wyryn's theory, it is mine," defended Tika before Wyryn could say a word. "Wizardelven have been trying all my life to solve this weakening, and it has reached a crisis. I do not ask for your belief, only your permission to follow the Line of Power which at least two Wizardelven have confirmed does indeed exist."

"Wise elven determined millennia ago that it was not safe to leave the Village," said Wizardelf Turva, who was in charge of Schooling. Her white hair was drawn back into a severe knot, and her eyes, once blue, were now so pale as to be almost colorless. She had always frightened Tika a little. Today, she had made her disapproval obvious from the beginning.

"This is not about safe or not," said Elder Moffa. "It's about solving– "

"Going wandering will not solve anything!" interrupted Elder Pilk, his dark eyes glaring. "This elfling has been called Wizardelf for one day, and already she has us at each others' throats! I say, remove her Authority, and let her take her place among the Apprentices. In five or ten years, she might have the wisdom to match her talent with Magik. I call for a Vote!"

Voices began to shout from around the table, and Tika sat looking at her hands and wondering what to do. She didn't want to cause such strife among elven. It would be better to go with their approval and support, but she didn't actually need it. She glanced at M'raj and Moog, sitting silently beside her. Even after experiencing the Line of Power for themselves, why should they side with her?

She stood. All eyes turned toward her, and the room was suddenly silent. "Please, Wizardelven. I do not wish to quarrel. I withdraw my suggestion. Perhaps our weakening of Powers has nothing to do with Lines of Power. What I now request, if Wizardelf Pilk will agree to withdraw his Vote demand, is to retain my Authority, and study the problem in more detail before proposing any other solution. Agreed?"

Everyone turned to Pilk. His ears, which had been folded back in anger, now twisted sideways in anxiety. Even beneath his dark skin, the blush of red could be seen. He cleared his throat. "Well, now . . . I am glad to see common sense has prevailed after all … I withdraw my request to remove Tika's Authority." He glanced around the room, seeing heads nodding in agreement. "So that's that, then. Let's proceed to the next order of business. Wyryn, you were requesting we train more Healers?"

Chapter Seventeen: The Quest Begins

A few days later, in the utter silence before dawn, Tika crept down the stairs, pulled her cloak around her shoulders, and took one last look at the warm and cozy kitchen of her elfling home. She put the note she had written, explaining what she felt she had to do, on the kitchen table. She doubted she would ever see her home again. What she was about to do was no doubt dangerous, and probably foolhardy. Still, she had no choice. The Wizardelven were never going to agree to let her go, and she knew, with a certainty that was impossible to explain, that the answers elven sought lay away from the Village.

Tika had been ready to go for several days, but had found excuses to stay. She hadn't slept at all this past night, though, and had realized there was no excuse to delay any longer.

Turning her back on her elflinghood, she snuck out the back door. Though it was extremely unlikely anyone would be awake at this time, she kept to the shadows on her way to the stable.

Once inside, Tika dug under the pile of hay in the loft to retrieve the saddlebags she had packed, and then dragged the heavy bags down the steps toward the stall where her pony, Blaize, was waiting. She greeted her friend with an apple and a scratch behind the ears, and the pony nuzzled her affectionately in return.

But when she tried to lift the saddlebags over the pony's back, they were too heavy. She was about to give up and unload some of the supplies she had been secretly packing for the past week, when the bags suddenly became much lighter.

"What –?" she exclaimed.

"Shhhh," said M'raj from the other side of the bags. "You'll wake the world!"

"M'raj! What are you doing here?" Tika whispered fiercely.

"You didn't think I would let you go off down the Valley alone, did you?" M'raj had come around the pony to cinch the saddlebag strap under the pony's belly expertly. When the strap was perfectly tight, she knew to knee the little mare in the tummy to force her to let out the breath she was holding, so that the strap could be tightened another couple of notches and not slip sideways.

Even in the dim dawn light, Tika could see the sparkle of mischief in her friend's eyes. "How did you know –?" she began.

"Oh, come on. Tika the Willful, Tika the Stubborn, giving up?" She grinned. "I knew what you were doing the minute I heard you give in. I've been sleeping here every night since, so you wouldn't leave without me."

"But – how come you believe me? How come you're here?"

"I won't say I understand, or even that I totally believe you," admitted M'raj. "But I've looked and looked at the Ley Lines map, and you're right; they don't look natural to me." Her eyes grew more serious. "And that Line does look like it leads off down the valley. I walked half a day yesterday, following the Line that you taught me to feel, and it just keeps going. So I came back here to wait for you to head off on your pony." She smiled. "Took you long enough."

"I had to pack . . . Are you packed?" Tika could hardly believe her eyes, or ears.

"Sure," M'raj said, ears twitching with humor. She left the stall, returning a few moments later leading her pony, a lovely dappled gray with saddlebags stuffed full.

"I'm packed too," said a deeper voice from the shadows of another stall. The stall door opened and Moog stepped out, leading a black pony.

"What?? Moog?? What are you doing here?" Tika exclaimed before the other two shushed her.

"Same as M'raj, apparently. I knew you were going to go with or without Council approval. And, as far as I can tell, nobody has a better suggestion about fixing the Power. I didn't know M'raj was coming, but I thought two elveens were better than one, and now I think three are better than two." He smiled at M'raj in a friendly way, walking closer.

M'raj smiled shyly but said nothing.

"Cute pony," Tika said. "What's his name? My pony is Blaize because of the white patch on her forehead, and M'raj's pony is called Forest because her coat looks like the dappled sunlight on the forest floor."

"Cool," said Moog, bowing to each of the ponies as if they were Wizardelven. He brought his pony closer. "M'raj, this is Mooky; Mooky, this is my new friend M'raj." Elveen and pony looked at one another for a moment, then the pony allowed M'raj to scratch behind his ears and they were friends.

"Mooky?" smiled Tika. "Moog and Mooky?" Every elf was given a foal while still a baby, for elven depended on their ponies for carrying heavy loads, as well as help with planting and harvesting crops. So young elflings' ponies were named by their parentgroup.

"My parentgroup have a strange sense of humor," explained Moog, his orange eyebrows waggling comically. Tika had to stifle her giggles.

With her friends' help, Tika soon had Blaize tacked up and ready to go. Not a moment too soon, either, for the sun was rising above the horizon and other elven would soon be rising as well.

The three elveens, who had suddenly become allies, led their ponies silently through the Village. With the ponies laden down with supplies, they knew it wasn't wise to ride them. All three elveens were wrapped up in their own thoughts, so there was little conversation as they left the Village and headed out into the Valley. Tika led, because she could follow the Line of Power without closing her eyes.

The going wasn't too hard, even without a path to walk on, because the land at this part of the Valley was fairly flat, and the three elven were walking through meadows. This early in the summer, the grass wasn't very tall, which also helped. The morning air was cool, but they knew it would be quite warm by the middle of the day, and walking kept them warm in the meantime.

Half a day later, they found themselves as far as any had ever been from home, at the ancient apple orchard which was one of Tika's favorite retreats. Even when there were no ripe apples to eat, Tika had always loved to climb the old trees. One in particular had a 'Y' of branches at the top, which had long provided a lovely relaxing seat for Tika to sit in and dream, swaying gently in the breeze.

While they let their ponies drink from the nearby stream, Tika placed her hand on the trunk of her favorite tree and said a silent goodbye. This abandoned orchard had, in fact, been one of the things that made Tika sure elven hadn't always lived only in the Village, for the trees had obviously once been planted in rows. It was just that elven didn't usually travel this far to harvest the apples because there were younger, more fruitful orchards closer to home.

When a hand suddenly came to rest on Tika's shoulder, she reached up to place her own on top. "Thanks, M'raj," she began, turning around – and then jumped back as though stung.

"Ha, Tika," said Br'on amiably. His smile was wider for M'raj. "Ha, M'raj … Nice day for traveling, isn't it?"

Suddenly, Moog was at her side. "What are you doing here, Br'on?" he asked harshly. M'raj came over, staring at Br'on silently.

Ignoring Moog, Br'on said, "Tika, you didn't think I'd let a dweeb like you go out into the wilderness alone, did you? You wouldn't have lasted a week." Behind Br'on was a heavily-laden pony. "And if I'd known these other dweebs were coming with you, I'd have packed a lot more food," he added, smirking at Moog.

Tika again wondered what Br'on had against Moog. But she wasn't about to get into it right now. "How did you know I – we – were leaving?" stammered Tika.

"Every elfling and elveen who knows you knew something was up when we heard you'd actually backed down on your idea. I've been expecting you to bolt, so I've been sneaking out here every day. What took you so long?" He was grinning quite smugly, and Tika felt anger rising.

"Just who do you think you are, Br'on Lleyn? Who asked for your help?" Tika stepped back from Moog and M'raj as well. "Who needs ANY of you? This is my plan, and no one else needs to take any risks. So just go home, all of you!" Thunder rumbled from the scattered clouds, and Br'on glanced up and began to worry about lightning.

Then he, M'raj and Moog looked at each other, shrugged, and seemed to come to a silent agreement for, taking their ponies by their lead ropes, they turned and began to head back toward the Village. Pride fought with practicality only for a moment or two, before Tika shouted, "Okay! All right! I *do* need your help! Please don't go!"

They turned back, and Tika saw Moog smile at Br'on, who smiled back for a moment before he remembered who he was looking at, and the smile faded. When the elveens were face to face once more, Tika tried to make peace by asking Br'on what his pony's name was.

"Nu," said Br'on with obvious affection, rubbing the dappled gray behind its ears. Then he became serious once more. He reached into his saddlebags and pulled out a number of items.

"Do you want to know what use I'll be?" he asked. "I'll tell you. Since Wizardelven were busy NOT solving the problem, I thought it might be wise, over the last couple of years, to learn how to do things without Magik in case it ever failed completely. Being in the Smelters Guild gave me a few ideas, and the rest I learned from Net. One of the things I've learned is how to make weapons to protect us." Br'on proudly held up his creations.

Tika noticed the resentment in Br'on's voice when he spoke of Wizardelven and wondered if this was the source of his jealousy of Moog. "Uh . . . you're going to protect us with a stick tied with a string, and some smaller sticks with metal melted onto their ends? – And what's that other thing that looks like an overgrown knife?" she said.

Br'on snorted in disgust, and put his weapons back in his saddlebag. "Okay, laugh if you want, but there may come a time when you'll be glad for my 'sticks' and 'knife'." He turned his pony around. "So, great and powerful Wizardelf, lead us along the Line."

Tika thought about apologizing and then gave up. After all Br'on had done to her over the last couple of years, she didn't owe him a thing. She wished, in fact, that it had been anyone but Br'on who had decided to come along. Still, she had to admit, four elven were probably safer than three, and Br'on stood half a head taller than Moog and M'raj, while she herself barely came to Br'on's chest. She did feel safer with him along, weird weapons or no.

As the traveled, Tika had no trouble following the Line of Power, but she noticed, as she had during previous excursions to the abandoned orchard, that the smaller side conduits extending from it grew fewer and fewer as they moved farther from the Village.

This worried her. If Magik was failing in the Village, with so many Lines, what would happen out here, with only one? The farther they got from the Village, the less connection she had with Net, too. It reminded her of her imprisonment in the Fair'day cave. As annoying as Fyr'wall had often been, and as frustrating as Proxy was, she couldn't imagine living – as she knew all other elven did – in a world empty of

Net. And now it looked like she was about to find out what that felt like!

She shivered with anxiety, but didn't mention her fears to the other elveens, who appeared to be in high spirits, excited by their adventure.

Finally, about the time they decided to stop for the night, the only Line left was the main one she had been able to coach Moog, M'raj and Wyryn into feeling. When she had offered to teach Br'on to feel the Line, he had scoffed.

"No, genius, I'll just follow along," he had said, shrugging. "I don't need much Magik to feel useful."

They stopped where a tall cliff rose up on the far side of a small river.

"This would be a good place to sleep tonight," said Br'on. "We could use the cliff at our back as protection against wild animals."

Tika had to agree. The sand along the opposite bank seemed a good place for cookstones, and there was ample water for the ponies. Grass grew along the riverbank, so the ponies could feed, as well.

"Then let's go!" grinned Moog, climbing onto his pony to cross the shallow stream. M'raj, Tika and Br'on followed.

Midstream, Moog's pony stumbled in a dip on the river bottom, and Moog had to grip the pony's mane to stay on. He turned to face the elven following him.

"Be careful of that spot just there," he warned. "It's a bit uneven." Just then, his pony stumbled again, and this time Moog tumbled off face first into the icy water. Splash!

"Ooo! Ow! Cold!" Moog shouted as soon as he was able to stand. The rocks on the bottom were slippery, and he slipped and stumbled as he finished crossing the river. His pony Mooky had wisely continued on, and stood watching him calmly from the far bank, his tail twitching from side to side in amusement.

Tika put a hand over her mouth to hide her smile, but Br'on didn't bother. "Hey, Accident, if you're done goofing around, you'd better get out of that water before you freeze to death!" he laughed.

Once safely on the far bank, all four elveens found themselves exhausted from a long day of unaccustomed travel. They wanted only to sit down and have something to eat and drink. However, after Moog had changed out of his wet clothes, all of the elveens first removed their ponies' burdens as they had all been taught, rubbed them down with some of the sand and grass from the river's edge, and then set them free to eat and drink.

Ponies and elven who bonded in their youth were never likely to stray far from one another. It was a partnership that went beyond master and beast.

Though her skin was sunburned and her feet blistered, Tika was proud of herself. If older elven were telling the truth, no elf had been this far from the Village anytime within their history. She felt brave and clever, doing something so strange and possibly dangerous.

Tika didn't feel so clever a few moments later, though, when she tried to heat cookstones so Moog could warm up. Concentrating on a pile of wide, flat rocks similar to those in every kitchen in the Village, she Sent the Hex to heat cookstones. Nothing happened. She Sent a stronger Hex. Nothing. Tika could sense the Line of Power was beneath the stones, so her Hex SHOULD be working!

She turned to M'raj, and said quietly, hoping Br'on wouldn't hear, "Can you heat the cookstones, M'raj? My Magik doesn't seem to be working."

She pointed to the pile of rocks, and saw M'raj's wild blue eyebrows furrow in concentration. But nothing happened. The rocks didn't even begin to glow. They looked at each other in dismay and embarrassment.

Finally, Tika said, "Br'on, could you heat these cookstones, please?" She didn't think it was necessary to tell Br'on about their failures. Perhaps he need never find out.

Br'on looked at her resentfully for a moment, and then focused on the pile for a moment or two, before saying, "It's as I suspected. Our Magik is even weaker out here, just as Tika's always was away from the Village. We won't be using Magik to heat cookstones from here on out, I'd say."

"– But I'm freezing!" said Moog, coming over while still rubbing his wet hair with a clean tunic before putting it on. "– Besides, we need cookstones! We have to cook our food! What are we going to do?"

"You're lucky I'm here," said Br'on smugly. "Another thing I've Queried Net about was how to cook food without Magik." He went over to where their bags lay at the foot of the cliff, and dug into one for a moment, returning with two rocks.

"There are lots of rocks here already," said Tika impatiently. "Are those Magikal rocks?" There were, of course, no such things, except in elfling stories.

"I'll need your help," said Br'on, ignoring the sarcasm. "We have to gather up some dried grass, the finer the better, as well as some sticks, from tiny to large. Pile them over here, by the rocks, okay?"

Puzzled, but curious to see how Br'on planned to work this non-Magikal magik, Tika, M'raj and Moog did as he requested and gathered grass and sticks. Looking through the sticks they had brought, though, Br'on called for them to stop, and sorted the sticks into two piles.

"I'm sorry," he told them, "I forgot to tell you to bring only dry sticks – old dead sticks. I'm not sure why, but Net said green sticks or wet sticks will not make fire."

"Sort of like a forest fire," mused M'raj to Tika as they went in search of the right kind of sticks. "Remember last fall, how the woods west of the Village were burning? And the old, dry trees on the ground burned the fastest?"

Tika nodded, remembering how frightening the flames had been. "I hope that is not what Br'on plans to do here," she said.

When they returned a few minutes later with two armloads of dry sticks, M'raj and Tika found Br'on and Moog had rearranged some rocks into a circle, with sand in the middle. Here they had piled the finest of the grass and the smallest of the twigs.

"Put them there, thanks," Br'on said over his shoulder, continuing to arrange the items within the circle.

"Looks like a complicated Hex, if you ask me," commented Tika.

"It's not a Hex at all," said Br'on, "and I've never actually done this before. I only Accessed the Knowledge on Net this week, when I knew we were leaving the Village. I didn't want to experiment inside the Village. Was afraid I might set fire to the whole town, or get in trouble with the Wizardelven."

"Then how come you're so sure this will work?" demanded Tika.

"Um . . . actually I'm not," said Br'on, giving her a dirty look. "Still, unless you have a better idea –?"

Tika and M'raj both shook their heads, and crouched on the other side of the circle of stones to watch.

"Is there anything else I can do to help?" asked Moog.

"I don't think so," said Br'on. "You'd better not get too close, because I'm not sure how fast the fire will get big – if it starts at all." He sighed, somewhat sorry he had sounded so smug earlier.

After moving back a bit, Tika, Moog and M'raj watched as Br'on took his two rocks out of a pocket and held one of them close to the twigs and grass.

"Will any two rocks do?" asked Tika.

"No, it took me hours to find the right kind," responded Br'on. "I had to go all the way to the lake to find them. They're called 'flint', I think. – Now please be quiet so I can concentrate."

Br'on began to strike one rock with the other. After changing the angle of his wrist several times, Br'on was able to strike a spark.

"Wow!" said Tika. "That's amazing. And you're not doing it with your Mind, just your hands?"

"I'm trying," said Br'on, striking spark after spark without lighting the grass or twigs. Hot sparks would land on them, and turn them brown, but the fire wouldn't start. "Darn!" Tired when he began, he was amazed how quickly the effort of banging stones together made his arms ache.

"Want me to try for a minute?" offered Moog.

Br'on looked angry, then shrugged and handed over the stones. Moog crouched beside the fire pit, striking the stones together as he had seen Br'on do. He was no more successful, until a small breeze blew across the circle as he sparked the rocks. For a moment, some of the grasses glowed red, and all of the other elveens cheered. But the breeze dropped away, and the embers faded almost instantly.

"What went wrong?" asked Br'on. "I thought you had it going!"

"I'm not sure," said Moog.

"I think it had something to do with the wind," said Tika. "Perhaps it's part of the Hex."

"It's not a Hex," insisted Br'on. "But I think you're right. Maybe fire does need wind. Here, Moog, let me have the stones again."

Moog handed over the stones, and sat back to watch. Br'on carefully sparked the rocks close to the grasses, and then when the spark jumped, blew on them at the same time. The embers grew bright red, but Br'on had blown so hard he was quickly out of breath, and the embers faded away again.

"Maybe we need a steady, gentle wind," suggested Tika, kneeling beside the pit. "Now try."

As Br'on sparked the stones, Tika blew a gentle, constant stream across the grasses. The embers began to glow red again. When M'raj could see her running out of air, she knelt down and began to blow, too. Smoke was beginning to rise. Then it blew into Tika's face, and she coughed loudly, scattering the embers, which quickly faded once more.

"Sorry," she murmured, her ears pink with embarrassment.

"That's okay," sighed Br'on. "We'll try again. Only this time, both of you keep the wind at your back."

While Br'on rearranged the small pile of grasses and twigs, the other two elveens moved until they were closer to him. Then all three repeated their technique. After several tries, they had a small fire going. Putting down his rocks, Br'on picked up slighting bigger twigs, and laid them gently on top. When M'raj and Tika picked up sticks to help, though, Br'on raised his hand to stop them.

"No," he said, "I think this part needs to be done carefully. It's like it's a baby fire, see? And a baby fire can only eat tiny twigs. I have to let the fire grow, gradually feeding it bigger and bigger twigs, until it's a real fire. Then we'll take turns feeding it, okay?"

M'raj and Tika nodded, and put down their sticks. Tika felt mildly jealous of Br'on as the fire-feeder, but she knew they wouldn't have had a fire without him. She gestured to M'raj and Moog, and the three of them went to the saddlebags to get some of the food they had brought from home. Br'on went to his saddlebag and pulled out a metal frying pan, black and thicker than any of them had ever seen. He set it carefully at the edge of the fire, where the rocks were already hot.

"Wow!" said Tika. "Where did you get that frying pan? I've never seen one like that."

"I made it," said Br'on proudly. "Net told me how ... Now, who wants scrambled eggs?" He brought out a bowl and a sack stuffed with straw and eggs. He started cracking eggs into the bowl.

"Two, please," said Tika, glancing curiously at M'raj, who nodded. "And two for M'raj."

"Can I have five?" asked Moog "... I don't know about you, but I'm dying of hunger!"

Tika burst out laughing, remembering his other nickname.

"Okay, fine, but I really am hungry. Aren't you, after all that walking?"

"Yes," admitted Tika, still giggling. "I just hope you packed a lot of food! In fact, let's pool our food for a celebration feast!"

All of the elveens had brought a wide, low, eating bowl as well as a fork, knife, spoon and mug. Moog brought out a loaf of bread and some cheese. Tika added some smoked meat she had smuggled out of the storeroom, and M'raj added buns and apples.

"If we're gone long enough, we're going to have to find our own food," commented Br'on as he expertly scrambled eggs in the frying pan.

"Find?" asked Tika.

"Yes," said Br'on, sounding superior. "I looked that up on Net as well. Apparently, this time of year we might be able to find bird's eggs. Other than that, I've memorized a list of types of plants that are okay for elven to eat, and where we might find them. I could even use my weapons to hunt a small animal, if we needed."

"Ew," said Tika, wrinkling her nose in disgust. "Who do you think would prepare it for eating?" She turned to M'raj. "Isn't your SoulFather a butcher? Have you ever done it? Do you think you could do it out here if we had to?"

M'raj nodded three times, though she didn't look happy. Glancing over as M'raj nodded, Br'on smiled at her with new respect, as if M'raj were now on the side of the doers rather than just the thinkers.

Tika was amazed at the skills she was discovering in her companions. When she had decided to set out, things like learning how to start a fire had never occurred to her, let alone how to find food in the wilderness. Her parentgroup had once tried to teach Tika to cook, but her lack of interest had ended in burned and wasted food, and they had soon given up.

"I don't even know how to cook," she admitted to the other elveens. "I'm sorry. This was all my idea, and it seems I'm not going to be very useful after all."

"Forget it," said Br'on.

"Yeah," agreed Moog. "You're the one who can trace the Line of Power. If we didn't think that was a good idea, we wouldn't be here." He glanced at Br'on and M'raj for confirmation, and Br'on nodded, though he was here in spite of, rather than because of, what he thought of Tika's idea. The way he saw it, he owed her a lot for the bullyings he had given her. This was his way of paying that debt. And he liked Tika's tall friend, M'raj. She was kinda cute with her blue hair. As for Moog, perhaps he wasn't such a dweeb after all.

"I can't believe no one's gone exploring like this before!" Moog added. He looked around. "I feel wonderful! It's so beautiful here."

The others agreed, but Tika wished there wasn't such a desperate reason for their Adventure. Still, they were here now, so there was no reason not to enjoy themselves! Once they had cooked and eaten supper, Tika took their dishes to the river and cleaned them, her way of showing gratitude for the other elven's efforts. It was important for everyone to pitch in, she thought.

'Hey,' she realized as she washed, '*maybe we're becoming friends. Who'd have thought that? M'raj, sure. But the bully and the fellow Apprentice who resented my Graduation?'* As she brought the clean dishes back to their camp site, she decided not to say anything about this to the others – no need to remind anyone of the reasons why they shouldn't like each other.

The sun was going down behind the mountains, glittering on the slowly-moving river like the lights at CenOps. As the light diminished, so did the birdsong, until the only sounds came from crickets. None of the elveens spoke. They were all exhausted, but proud of themselves. Such brave adventurers!

After putting several logs onto the fire to keep it going overnight, the four elveens pulled their blankets around themselves and lay down. For a long time, none of them slept, despite how tired they were.

Although elveens occasionally slept outside overnight, none of the four had been this far from home in their lives. As pleased as they were at how far they'd come, and at how much they'd achieved on their first day, while they lay trying to get to sleep, their initial excitement was changing to anxiety about what lay ahead.

Tika worried about her inability to heat cookstones. While it might be only temporary, it upset her more than she had let on to her companions. All her life, she had been gifted in Magik, recognized as a special elfling, and given privileges other elflings were denied. She had taken all of this for granted. But what if she couldn't solve the problem causing the loss of Power? What if she had to go home and live like other elven? What would she be without Magik? Trying to see herself through others' eyes, all Tika could see was a fifteen-year-old elfling, small for her age, who was unused to working hard at anything.

Watching Br'on make a fire had showed her just how useless she might be in a world without Magik. Br'on was younger than Moog, even if he was bigger and stronger. And she was younger than all of them! Aside from her Magikal gifts, she had little to offer the others. And that wasn't the worst of their troubles.

Tika hadn't mentioned it to the others, but she had realized that the path was going to be harder to follow tomorrow. The meadows were giving way to trees, and the Line seemed to be following the river right through the forest. Beneath the tall pine, ash, and maple trees Tika recognized, there was an undergrowth of scrub. From previous experience in the woods closer to the Village, she suspected there would be brambles, too. It would be easier to go around somehow, but she wasn't sure from what distance she'd still be able to sense the Line.

Tika debated turning around. Was she crazy, leading these courageous elveens and their ponies into the unknown? If she went home, so would they. She was sure that relief would outweigh anger among their parentgroups, and they might not even be punished very badly.

Then she contemplated sneaking out at first light and continuing her Quest alone. No need for the other three to risk their lives. As she finally drifted into sleep, she made up her mind to do just that.

Chapter Eighteen: Followed?

As it turned out, it was full daylight when Tika awoke. She jumped out of her blanket, then moaned as her stiff and sore legs complained about the effort. She was still a bit fuzzy, thinking she should hurry up and get going before the other elveens awoke.

Then she noticed none of the elveens were where they had lain the previous night. She twirled around, and found herself grateful for the nearby cliff wall as dizziness overtook her. She thought she might fall down, but there was a steadying hand on her arm.

"Are you all right?" M'raj asked.

"Um, yes, I guess so," said Tika shakily. "Where's Br'on?"

"Over there, loading up the ponies," said M'raj, smiling. "We thought you were going to sleep all day!" She let go of Tika's arm when she saw her friend had her balance back. "Breakfast is on that rock there, but I suggest you eat quickly, because we're anxious to get going."

Tika saw that she'd missed her chance to leave them behind, and decided not to drag them along for another whole day. She and M'raj walked over to join the other two beside the ponies.

"Listen, guys," she said around a mouthful of food (quite good, she noticed). "I really think the three of you should go back to the Village. I'm not sure what I'm doing out here. All I know is I can't quit. But that doesn't mean you have to take these chances. You've got parentgroups who are worried about you, friends and work waiting for you . . ." She stopped when she saw their ears fold backward.

"You arrogant brat!" spat Br'on. "What makes you think this quest is any less important to us than to you? I won't speak for M'raj or Moog, but there's no way I'm going to give up, even if I have to learn to follow the Line of Power myself. The whole Village may be depending on this trip, and you want all the glory for yourself!"

"It's not like that, Br'on," Tika tried to explain.

"Are you sure?" asked Moog. "Maybe you just don't like it that there are things we mere mortal elven can do that your Magikal genius can't." The way Br'on smiled at him at that suggested the two elveens had decided on some kind of truce, spoken or unspoken.

"Tika, all of us CHOSE to be here," murmured M'raj in her ear, putting her arms around Tika. "We're NOT quitting."

"Okay, okay, I can see I'm outnumbered," Tika said after gratefully returning the hug.

"Good," said Br'on.

"Yes," said Moog. "Now don't bring it up again, okay?" He glanced at Br'on for support, who nodded in agreement.

"Yeah, and no sneaking off while we're asleep, either," Br'on added, making Tika wonder if he had Heard her thoughts, though she had been careful not to Send them.

"Okay, okay. I won't sneak off," said Tika.

"Promise?"

"Promise." It was a promise Tika was relieved to make, if she were being honest with herself.

"Good, then, that's settled," said Br'on. "Now finish your breakfast and let's get going."

While Tika wolfed the last of her food, she felt the lightest of MindTouches. She glanced around to see who was reaching out to her. First, she saw M'raj try to teach Br'on how to sense the Line. M'raj could find it as long as she closed her eyes, and she had Br'on trying her dowsing technique of holding at y-shaped stick of wood in front of him while he walked around.

As usual, M'raj was silent, directing Br'on with her hands. Tika wondered if her friend would ever start talking within the group.

Br'on looked foolish wandering back and forth, eyes closed, arms stretched in front like an elf suddenly gone blind. His hands never pulled down toward the Line as Wyryn's had, though. Tika was sorry, because it would have been nice to have everyone's help in sensing the Line, and it would have helped Br'on to believe her when she said she sensed it.

So the MindTouch wasn't coming from M'raj or Br'on. She glanced the other way. Moog was shoving his things into his saddlebags carelessly. He didn't seem to be even aware of her, so it wasn't him, either.

She shivered. *Who was near enough to reach out to her? Maybe she had imagined it!*

Because she wasn't sure it had even really happened, she didn't say a word to the others as she stashed her blanket and personal things back in Blaize's saddle bags and picked up the lead rope, hoping to shake off the uneasy feeling that had come over her. The other three elven and their ponies followed behind as Tika continued to follow the Line of Power, picking her way through the trees beside the river and avoiding the brambles as best she could. Still, she knew their clothes, and the ponies' hides, were getting nasty scratches. This was much harder going than the previous day, and all of them were soon tired.

One of things making her tired was that every step they took made Net less and less Accessible. Now it was like a very distant voice, and there were no answers when she Sent a Query. As she had felt in the cave, the absence of Net from her Mind made her sick with anxiety. She thought she would rather lose an arm or a leg than Net. She had assumed that Net was attached to the Lines of Power, and that as long as she was near a Line, she would have Access to it. But now she realized that Net was, in fact, attached to CenOps, and that soon she would be just like every other elf, deaf to Net.

This, more than anything else, made her want to turn around and go home – go back to the place where she was super Magikal, and knew so many things that other elven didn't. It was especially painful after having been granted Sup'rvis Authorization less than a week earlier. All the Queries she wanted to make!

She reminded herself that this Quest was more important than she was – more important than any of them. Each of them had sacrificed a lot to be out here – not just her!

Just the same, after only a couple of hours, she led them back toward the river, which they could hear gurgling nearby, so they and the ponies could get a drink. The water was still icy at this time of year, so they couldn't walk in the stream, but it tasted wonderful. Tika splashed some on her hot face, and rubbed the back of her neck with more. Her long hair was heavy with sweat. How she wished she could have a long, cool bath and wash her hair!

Although every elf's life in the Village was busy, and elflings and elveens participated in physical fitness programs at School, none of the four elveens had walked this far in their lives. Tika's muscles were screaming in protest, and her feet were burning. She was tempted to soak her boots in the water. Moog had obviously had the same thought and had waded knee-deep into the stream, some cheese in one hand and an apple in the other. He was munching contentedly while he cooled his feet.

"Do your feet burn, too?" she asked him.

"Do they ever!" said Moog, wading back out. "But it gets cold pretty fast. I think that's about enough for now." He sat down and dumped water from each boot before putting the boots back on.

"Mine, too," said Br'on from where he was sitting on a rock. "But I'm not sure it's a good idea to walk in wet boots, Moog. Did you bring another pair?"

"No," said Moog. "It never occurred to me. Did you?"

"No," sighed Br'on. "It's pretty hard to imagine what you'll need when you're doing something no elf has ever done before."

M'raj took off her boots and dipped her bare feet in the stream, gasping with shock at how cold the water was.

They were silent for a few minutes. Tika, for one, wanted only to climb into her own little bed, pull her blankets up, sleep for a week, and forget this whole thing had ever happened. Instead, she stood up, picked up Blaize's reins, and walked along the bank. She could barely sense the Line from here, but the going was a bit easier. The other elveens quickly put their boots back on and followed her, leading their ponies.

An hour later, the sky began to darken, threatening rain. Again Tika stopped. M'raj said to her quietly, "You're supposed to be good with Weather. Can you get rid of those clouds?"

"I can try," Tika said tiredly, careful not to look at Br'on, who had experienced her control of weather in less friendly circumstances. She turned her face to the sky, and closed her eyes. After a moment or two, she opened them again. "Guys, I can't Sense the Weather Sat."

"Maybe you need to be closer to the Line of Power," Moog suggested.

"Hmmm," said Tika. "Br'on, could you and Moog wait here with the ponies while M'raj and I go back to the Line?" Tika knew there was some kind of connection between Magik and the Lines, but she wasn't completely sure how it related to the Weather Sat. Still, it was the only thing she could think to suggest at the moment.

"Sure," grimaced Br'on. "Glad to sit for a few minutes."

"Won't be sitting for very long, I'm afraid," Tika said. "Come on, M'raj."

The two elveens struggled back through the undergrowth to where Tika could feel the Line's Power getting stronger.

"Here," she said, sitting on a fallen tree and looking down at her feet. "Can you feel it?"

M'raj closed her eyes and put her hands out. "Yes, it actually feels stronger here than in the Village!" Her eyes opened wide in surprise.

"Really? Good. Now try to Feel the Weather Sat."

"Me?" M'raj's voice came out as a squeak.

"Yes. I think one of the things holding elven back from solving this problem is that we've been stuck in tradition. Just because you're in the Monitors Guild doesn't mean you can't Control weather." Tika spoke with more confidence than she felt, but as the words came out of her mouth, her ears had to agree.

They needed to break out of the traditions and restrictions that had been limiting them! She had been really impressed with Br'on for researching how to do things without Magik. That had simply never occurred to her because Magik came so easily to her. But now she realized that her Magik was as good as gone – which was all the more reason to find out if the others had Powers they had never tried.

With a shrug, M'raj closed her eyes and turned her face toward the sky. Tika saw her lips moving, and smiled. Elveens were trained to say their Hexes inside their minds, and it indicated how hard M'raj was concentrating that she was unaware of the slip.

Through the tree branches, Tika watched the sky. Still gray. She kept quiet, not wanting to interrupt M'raj's Hex.

Finally, the gray thinned and then disappeared, and the sky was blue again.

"Hurray!" Tika said. "You did it, M'raj. Awesome!" She wasn't sure if her friend had actually contacted the Weather Sat or if the weather had just changed on its own, but she decided there was no reason to make her friend feel less confident.

M'raj opened her eyes, glancing up as if afraid of what she would see, and then grinning a comical grin. "Genius, that's what I am," she said, her ears turning bright pink.

"Yes, you are," Tika agreed, slapping her on the back. Then it happened again, that feeling of being watched or her Mind Touched.

"Did you feel that?" she asked M'raj. "Did you just feel a MindTouch?"

M'raj's eyebrows rose. "Nope. Nothing. Did YOU?"

"I – I think so," said Tika. "It's just – so faint – that I'm wondering if I'm imagining it."

"Oh! Is something making you nervous?"

Tika opened her mouth, and then closed it again. She was going to sound crazy. But this was M'raj! If she didn't trust her best friend, she couldn't trust anyone. "I … I'm wondering if – maybe – Xinar is following us, using the same technique that Wyryn used to track us down in the cave. You know, with delicate MindTouches?"

"Xinar?? No way! He's confined to the Fair'Day cave … He wouldn't – He couldn't! … Could he?"

"I'm not sure. This is the second time this has happened, but I don't have enough experience with MindTouches to be sure."

"Tika, it's natural to be nervous this far away from our families and friends. But – honestly! How could Xinar be following us? We left in secret! We packed supplies for a long journey. He couldn't have done that, too." M'raj's face was serious and her arms were crossed.

"Well," Tika replied quietly, "the three of you figured out that I was absolutely going to do this and were prepared before I was, actually. Don't you think it's possible that Xinar figured it out, too?"

The color drained from M'raj's face. "Well – um – yes, I suppose that's true … What do you want to do about it?"

Tika shrugged. "Nothing – for now. I don't have any proof, so I don't want to tell the others just yet. But I would feel better if you were helping me keep an eye out."

"Absolutely! I'll try to pay more attention to see if I'm also getting MindTouches, and I'll keep a lookout for any suspicious activity when we stop for the night … You aren't worried that he'll try to elfnap us again, are you?"

"No, what good would that do him now? I already told him that I don't know why my Powers are stronger than most. If he IS following us, he might think that I actually know where I'm going …"

Tika stuck out her tongue to show how little she actually knew about where they were headed, and then added, "Now let's get back to Br'on and Moog. I think they've had enough rest, wouldn't you say?"

As they walked back, M'raj asked, "Tika? What exactly IS a Weather Sat? Or maybe, WHERE is it? I've always just thought of the Weather Sat as a Hex, but if we get our Powers from the Lines in the ground, why do elven look to the sky when doing a Weather Hex?"

"Hmmm. Good question. Well, I guess we look to the sky because that's where weather comes from. As for what a Weather Sat is, or if it has a location other than Magikal, is another question for Net when we return." Since no one knew that she used to be able to Access Net anywhere she wanted, there was no point in complaining that she couldn't anymore. So they walked back in silence.

When they got back, though, they found Moog digging through his saddlebags.

"Hey, I didn't say we were ready to stop for the day," teased Tika. "What are you doing?"

"Finding these," announced Moog proudly, producing two straw harvesting hats. The simple woven hats were worn by elven working in the fields to keep the sun off their faces. They weren't the most beautiful pieces of apparel, but the tall-topped hats left lots of room for ears.

The trouble was, Tika saw, there were only two of them. Obviously, Moog had brought one for himself, and one for Tika, but he hadn't known M'raj or Br'on would be along. How could they share these fairly? All four had sunburns on their fair skins, and Tika's ears were blistered and sore. She would be grateful to have one of the ugly hats, but then who would have to do without?

Moog, it turned out, was a step ahead of her. He handed her and M'raj each a hat, and then before they could protest, turned around and picked something up from behind the rock he'd been sitting on.

From the wide grasses along the riverbank, Moog had fashioned two more hats for himself and Br'on. Although every elfling was taught how to make them, Moog's were obviously hastily done. They were, if such a thing were possible, even uglier than the ones he'd brought. But when he proudly slapped his onto his head and handed the other to Br'on, neither Tika nor M'raj laughed.

"It's okay to laugh," smiled Moog, watching their faces. "I know they're badly done. But my ears couldn't take any more sun, and since you two were determined to get rid of the first cloud-cover we've seen, I thought we could all use the protection."

"Thanks!" said Br'on and Tika at the same time, laughing. M'raj smiled her gratitude.

"I'm sure none of us looks exactly elegant at this point," said Tika. "And it's not likely to get better is it?" She picked at the hem of her beautiful blue-green tunic, so recently rescued from its mud bath by Wyryn's partner M'lina. Now it was torn and dirty.

"It doesn't matter," said Moog consolingly. "What we're doing is far more important than how we look doing it."

The rest of the day was slow going, and the elven made little progress. Moog regretted wetting his boots, for the backs of his heels were soon red and raw, and he found himself limping. Finally, they had to stop. After he removed his boots, Tika looked at the blisters on his feet. "Wyryn taught me a bit about Healing," she told him. "Can I try?"

"Please!" Moog didn't even joke about her learning things most elflings didn't.

Tika closed her eyes, and struggled to connect to the Line of Power. After a moment, though, she could feel the Power surging through her, and gently put a hand on each blister, imagining, as she'd learned to do, that the blister was shrinking and then gone. She resisted the urge to dive deeper to look for Dark Pieces. Now was not the time for that investigation!

While she worked, Br'on had been digging around in his saddlebags. By the time Moog was healed, Br'on had returned with some cloth and some string.

The other two elven looked at him in confusion. "What's that for?" Tika asked.

"Well, the ground is fairly soft here, so I think we should tie Moog's boots together and hang them over his pony's back to dry. And then he can wrap his feet in these waxed cloths that our cheese was in, and tie them with string to make temporary boots. What do you think?"

Almost before Br'on had finished talking, Moog had grabbed the cloth and string and was fitting them around his feet. He wrapped the cloth fairly loosely, so that his long feet had room to bend, and then used his utility knife to cut the strings into shorter lengths. He wrapped the strings around the cloth, tied them at his ankles, and then wound them up his calves and tied them again just under his knees in a fairly tight knot. "Brilliant!" he said happily. "Thanks, Br'on!"

While not perfect, cloth boots were better than wet boots, so the four elven moved ahead. Keeping to the river bank helped, and made it easy to find an appropriate spot to stop for the night. When the river turned, the bank widened into a small cove, a perfect place to camp.

Once again, the four companions unloaded their ponies, scrubbed the sweat off of them with sand and grass, and set them free to graze and drink.

Then the elven went searching for dry wood, and again, Br'on started a fire. There wasn't much conversation between the exhausted group while they ate. By the time Moog returned from taking his turn cleaning the dishes in the stream, he found M'raj, Br'on and Tika already asleep beside the fire. He piled a few more logs onto the fire, and then pulled his own blanket around him and was asleep almost before he lay his head down.

Which was probably why none of them heard the bandit in the night. When they woke up, however, they quickly realized they'd been vandalized. The contents of their saddlebags were spread across the sand, and the food was gone. Or mostly gone.

Tika felt like crying, and M'raj and Moog looked like they were feeling the same way. Br'on picked up what was left of an apple and examined it closely.

"An elf did this," he announced. "Look at these teeth marks."

"I left my saddlebags buckled up," said Moog, despairing the loss of his large cache of food. "What kind of elf would open them up?"

"Xinar," said M'raj and Tika at the same time.

"WHAT??" said Br'on and Moog. "Impossible!"

So Tika had to explain about the MindTouches and how she suspected that Xinar, and possibly his Apprentices, were following them.

Br'on was angry. "Why didn't you say something sooner? We could have kept watch!"

Tika blushed bright red. "I – I wasn't sure," she said. "I thought I felt his MindTouch once or twice, but it was so light, and so brief, that it was easy to think I had imagined it. I – didn't want to worry everyone over something that was just a suspicion. After what he put us through, I thought maybe I was just being paranoid. I'm still not entirely sure it was him."

"It's definitely possible, though," said Moog. "He's crazy enough to do this! And if he didn't pack enough food, maybe he's starving."

"Well, we'll definitely take turns keeping watch overnight from now on," said Br'on, sighing. "We should have been doing that anyway. Who knows what beasts might attack in the night?"

"Okay. So what do we do now?" said Moog.

The four elveens looked at each other. Then they began to pick up and repack their bags. Br'on found some bread and Moog found a couple of apples that had been underneath some other things. M'raj found some candy, and Tika a bit of cheese that, if you cut the bitten part off, could still be considered edible.

They pooled their meager feast, and ate.

"Looks like this is our last easy meal," said Tika finally. "Br'on, what was it you said about finding food?"

"I think we can do it," said Br'on, not sounding all that sure. "But it's going to slow us down even more. Did that red dragon, what's her name, give you any clue about how far we would have to go, Tika?"

"No," said Tika, shaking her head. "But the far end of the Valley can't be much more than a week's walk, right? Let's just hope the Source is within the Valley."

Br'on taught the other three elveens how to recognize well-disguised nests among the cattails at the river's edge, and they gathered as many eggs as they could. Though the boiled eggs tasted quite different from what they were used to, the four elveens gobbled them down hungrily, washing them down with water from the river.

Br'on also taught the others which plants were edible, and which had edible roots, so while their food tasted strange and sometimes bitter, they did not starve. It didn't take long, however, to get tired of eggs and roots for breakfast, lunch, and dinner. *Too bad it was still too early in the summer for berries and they were months away from fresh nuts,* thought Tika. Something else she should probably have thought about before starting on this quest!

As the days grew warmer, they took the opportunity to bathe together in a shallow spot in the river. No one thought twice about being naked in front of the others, since communal bathing was a normal part of their culture.

As she undressed with the others, Tika thought how her long, curly hair had become increasingly matted and harder to comb as the days went on. She hoped the shampoo she had brought along would be enough to make it manageable again.

But shivering in the still-cold river, Tika could not untangle her thick hair. The other elveens quickly bathed and got out, but Tika struggled and struggled. SoulMother Chan'ja usually helped her with it. She hadn't realized how much she would miss her parentgroup! Tears slid down her face as she finally climbed out, dressed in dry clothes from her saddlebags and sat on a rock to dry her hair.

The other elveens had gone off to collect edible plants. M'raj returned first, to find Tika crying, her hair a wretched tangle down to her waist. She stood awkwardly in front of her friend, not knowing what to say.

"You'll have to cut it off," said Tika in a voice so low M'raj could barely hear her. "I can't take proper care of it out here." She didn't look up.

"I could try to comb it out," suggested M'raj, though it looked worse than a wild pony's. "It might not be so bad." Everyone in the Village knew how proud Tika was of her hair. While she wasn't particularly vain, she had always refused to let her hair be cut, even when most of the other elveens, like M'raj, had cut theirs into the newest shorter styles.

"No," said Tika, a bit louder. "Just cut it, please. Now."

M'raj dug out her sharpest knife and managed to cut off the tangled mess. She tried to leave what was left an even length, but it still looked awful. The shorter Tika's hair was, the curlier it was, and so her shorn hair stood out from her head like a red ball of fuzz. It made the elveen want to laugh, if she hadn't been so sad for Tika's sake.

"Thank you," Tika said simply, blinking back tears, when M'raj announced she was finished. "I'm just glad I didn't think to bring a mirror." She took her comb, and ran it through the short hair. "Good. At least now I can comb it. Thanks." She smiled a brokenhearted smile and vowed never to mention her lost hair again.

When Moog and Br'on saw her, she could see them trying not to laugh. Then Br'on spoke up.

"Good thinking, Tika. Not only is shorter hair easier to care for, but summer is here now, and it's only going to get hotter … M'raj, I'm assuming you're the barber? Could you please cut my hair – as short as possible?" He pulled his long hair out of the hair tie and shook it out and then sat on a rock in front of M'raj.

"– Are you SURE?" M'raj asked, lifting his beautiful yellow hair as if it was a beautiful fabric.

"I'm sure," said Br'on with a smile that looked genuine.

Tika felt like crying again, but pushed her tongue under her top lip to prevent herself. It was such a kind gesture!

"I'm next!" announced Moog, sitting down next to Br'on and pulling off his straw hat so that his orange curls sprang free. "My hair is a rat's nest at the best of times. Shave it!"

"I'll have to sharpen my knife," said M'raj. "Give me a minute." She went over to her saddlebag for the whetstone they all carried. Every elf carried a knife and was taught how to handle it safely and how to sharpen it at a young age. "Tika, can you do Moog's while I do Br'on's?"

"Um … sure …" said Tika uncertainly, turning to go to her saddlebags for her knife and whetstone. "I'm not sure what to do," she admitted when she returned. She wished again that she had Access to Net to find out.

"I'm no hair stylist, but you just take a small portion of the hair, like this…" said M'raj, picking up a strand of Br'on's hair, "… and then you use your knife to cut it off." She ran the knife along the strand, close to Br'on's head but angled toward the ground. Her sharp knife sliced through the hair easily and she dropped the cut-off strand to the ground with a sigh, though she didn't say anything.

"Are you sure you trust me to do this?" Tika asked Moog, who had moved to sit on the ground so that she could reach his head more easily.

"Go for it," he said, but his eyes were closed. "I trust you."

After a few awkward moments, Tika got the hang of what she'd seen M'raj do, and within minutes, both elveens had shorn heads. They didn't look elegant, that was for sure!

"Oh-kay," announced Tika. "I – guess? – I'm done … Maybe it's a good thing we don't have a mirror?"

Everyone laughed as Br'on and Moog stood up, brushing stray hairs off their shoulders.

"Do mine," said M'raj suddenly, sitting in front of Tika. "We should all keep our hair short from now on, I think."

"Really? Your hair is pretty short already," said Tika. "I'm sure it's okay –" She gazed with admiration at M'raj's turquoise hair, which waved gently just below her ears.

"Nope! Just cut it all off," said M'raj. "I'm sure I'll feel more comfortable with shorter hair."

Tika wasn't sure if any of them really meant what they were saying, or if they were cutting their hair to make her feel less sad about the loss of her own coppery ringlets.

Regardless, once M'raj also looked like a sheep in shearing season, all four elveens realized they had to bathe again to get rid of the itchy hairs.

As she emerged from dunking underwater, Tika found herself splashed by M'raj.

"Hey now!" she said, angry. But seeing the mischief in M'raj's face, Tika's anger faded and she splashed M'raj back. Soon it turned into a water fight between all four elveens, and the sad feelings that any of them had about losing their long hair were drowned with laughter. Tika's heart swelled with gratitude.

The next ten days passed in a kind of blur, an endless repetition of placing one foot in front of the other. Despite keeping watch, there was no sign of Xinar. Tika continued to feel delicate MindTouches, but nothing more. She was pretty sure he was just following them to see where they were going. Or where she was leading them, actually. He was obsessed with her and her control of Magik. She sighed, thinking about how little Magik any of them had at this point. As long as he left them alone, there didn't seem to be anything anyone could do about him.

As the weeks went on, their muscles ceased to complain, and the blisters on their feet turned to calluses. Their hats kept their faces and ears from getting sunburned any worse, and it began to feel as if they had been together forever.

Eventually, though, the land began to rise again as they entered a dark forest. Muscles ached again from the steady uphill hike, but at least the forest was clear of brambles. Unfortunately, there were no more eggs to be found. Fortunately, they had gathered all they could as they left the plain, and had filled their saddlebags with eggs packed in grass.

Br'on reasoned not only would the grass help prevent the eggs from breaking, they could use the grass to start fires so they could cook the eggs. Tika was impressed with his wisdom. They also decided they would have to leave the egg-filled saddlebags on the ponies overnight in turns, to prevent the eggs from being stolen by Xinar or even small animals. Who knew what strange beasts lived out here, so far from the Village?

The river cut a path through the forest, but the bank was rocky and steep, and they had to move away from it, though they never went far from this source of drinking water. The Line of Power ran parallel to the river, so it was easy to Sense, but the climbing was hard and the forest was dark. It was hard to remain optimistic. Each of them felt homesick, but no one mentioned it.

Actually, there was very little conversation. The ponies, sturdy and sure-footed, had an easier time, and sometimes they had to drag their owners up particularly steep slopes. As the season progressed, though, they started to find edible berries that they recognized. What a treat!

C.A. MAVEN

Finally, a few days of climbing and trudging brought them out of the forest and onto a plateau. The four elveens stood together on the edge of the plateau and gazed down at the Valley, trying to see the Village.

"I've never been up this high before," said Moog. "Everything looks so TINY!" Up on the windy plain, his hair blew wildly around his head, making him look like a demon elf from elfling stories.

"I can't see the Village," said Br'on. "I'm not even sure where to look."

"Follow the river," said Tika, pointing to the glittering ribbon cutting across the bottom of the valley.

"That's the river??" Br'on exclaimed. "It looks like a silver thread from Father One's Celebration robe!"

"Well, it's the river," confirmed Tika. "I'm sure of it."

"I see the Village!" exclaimed Moog, pointing.

The other elveens followed his finger, and squinted.

"Are you sure?" said Br'on. "That's nothing but a blob!"

"No, I think he's right," said Tika, holding onto a nearby tree and leaning out as if that would bring the Village closer. Her voice became sad. "I can't believe it's so far away! Did we really walk all this way?"

"I still don't see it," complained Br'on. "And anyway, there's no point in thinking about it. Our focus is in the other direction, right?"

Tika shivered and turned away to hide the tears in her eyes. It was her fault they were all so far from home. Safe and comfortable in the Village, she had been SO sure that this was the right thing to do. But out here, with everyone she knew so very, very far away, she felt like a little elfling. She wished she could climb on Grandelf Dorinda's lap and hug her one more time. There was no point in turning back now, but what had she DONE??

142

Chapter Nineteen: The Abandoned Village

At least the going was easier on the broad, flat plain. With most of their food supplies gone, what was left could be loaded onto two of the ponies, so they took turns riding the other two.

During all this time, Tika, Moog and M'raj could feel the Line of Power growing slowly but steadily stronger. And with M'raj teaching him every day, even Br'on was starting to be able to feel it.

Tika was conflicted. On the one hand, she celebrated that her shy friend was stretching her wings. But on the other hand, it meant that she no longer had a special relationship with M'raj. In fact, M'raj seemed to want to spend more and more time with Br'on.

Well, maybe it was just friendship. They did not hold hands or kiss, Tika told herself. M'raj was the same age as she was. That was too young for romantic interest – wasn't it?? She shook off her jealous thought. *'Focus on the Quest!'* she told herself.

That night, they camped in front of a rocky outcropping at the edge of the forest on the far side of the plateau.

"How long have we been hiking?" Br'on asked, sipping his rose-hip tea, made from the large stash of dry leaves he'd brought along and shared with his friends.

Tika hadn't really thought about it, but Moog spoke up.

"We've seen two full moons since we started, and the moon is half now, so about two and a half months?"

"Wow!" said M'raj. "It's hard to believe! I had never been away from my parent group more than one night before we left. I couldn't imagine being away from them ... And now, I hardly think of them!" She blushed bright red.

"You, too?" said all of the other elveens at the same time. Then they looked at each other and everyone laughed.

"I guess it's really just part of growing up?" suggested M'raj. "I mean, we would all have left our parent groups eventually, right?"

"Of course!" said Br'on, placing a kind hand on M'raj's shoulder. He winked broadly. "Some of us sooner than the others!"

Everyone laughed again, but no one made eye contact. It was as if they were all suddenly aware of the possibility of forming their own parent group, and no one wanted to be the first to suggest that!

***

"Tika! Wake up!" whispered Moog.

Tika sat up, confused. It was still dark, though the sun was just starting to crack the horizon. "– What?"

"Shhh," said Moog. "Look!" He pointed beyond the dying fire to many sets of yellow eyes that gleamed in the firelight. Wild dogs??

Tika couldn't make out details of the beasts, but the animals were growling softly. Moog had gone and roused M'raj and Br'on.

"What do we do?" asked M'raj when they were all huddled together. "Add more wood to the fire?"

"We're out of wood," said Moog sadly. "And to get some, we'd have to get past – THEM."

"Get out your knives and keep your backs to the rocks," said Br'on, pulling out his long knife – which he called a 'sword' – and holding in with both hands.

A moment later, all four elveens had their backs to the rocks, side by side with their knives out in front of them. As it got lighter, Tika could make out that these were not wild dogs after all, but rather hairier cousins with long legs, big ears and a long jaw with protruding fangs. Their shoulders were as tall as Tika! She desperately wished she could access Net and find out what they were! And – more importantly – how to make them go away!!

"What do we do now? Wait for them to attack?" she whispered to Br'on at her side. He had his sword held out in front, but his hands were trembling, whether from fear or just the weight of the weapon, Tika wasn't sure.

"They probably just want food," said Moog from the other side of Br'on. "What can we give them?"

"I – I'm pretty sure they want US as food," whispered Tika. Tears slid down her cheeks. What a reckless way to die!

"Climb the rocks!" shouted M'raj suddenly.

While the others quickly turned to help one another up the rock pile, M'raj grabbed what was left of one of the logs, with the embers at the other end still glowing red, and charged the gathered animals. "Gah!" she screamed. "Go AWAY!!" She waved the log wildly, striking one of them on the head, causing it to yelp and run away. "Come ON!" she yelled, twisting and turning. "Come and GET me if you DARE!!"

She seemed to have no fear, and in a moment, Br'on had leapt down from the rocks with his sword. He yelled and waved the sword as wildly as M'raj had been waving the log.

He didn't connect with any of the animals but, confronted with two loud, crazy creatures, the pack decided to look for easier prey and turned as a group and took off into the forest.

A moment later, Tika and Moog had climbed down, too, and the four stood together, laughing and crying at the same time.

"I think you can drop the log now," Moog said softly to M'raj, whose eyes were still wild. He put a hand on her shoulder. "You saved us!"

"M'raj! Your hands!!" cried Tika as soon as M'raj dropped the log. "You're burned!"

"Oh, am I?" asked M'raj, looking down at her hands with a distant expression. Then she fainted.

While Br'on and Moog found more wood to add to the fire, Tika knelt beside her friend. She was actually grateful that M'raj was unconscious, so she couldn't feel pain. With the Power of the Line so much stronger here, it was fairly simple to Heal the burns, even though she was distracted and worried that the pack would come back soon.

When M'raj awoke an hour later, she seemed fine, but it was like she didn't remember the attack or her crazed response. Her hands were still a bit tender and pink, but she helped pack up their saddlebags as if nothing had happened.

"Are you okay?" Tika asked, worried.

"Yeah. Why wouldn't I be?" M'raj responded, sounding distant, like she was still in shock.

"Well – you SPOKE in front of the others!" Tika said.

"Oh. Did I? Well, these are my friends. I don't know why I've been holding back," said M'raj. Her eyes were a bit unfocused. "Right?"

Tika wasn't sure what to make of this, so she just shrugged and finished her own packing. All of them were exhausted from the stress of the attack, but they decided it was important to get as far away from this spot as possible.

The Line had looked like it was leading straight up the mountain, and Tika had despaired how either they or their ponies would manage. But as they approached the forest, the Line veered to the left. The four elveens had no choice but to follow, though they weren't happy to be leaving behind the river, with its bountiful drinking water. They filled their water sacks, as well as anything extra they'd brought that might hold water. Even though they worried about finding water, one of the benefits of being so near the forest was that they started to find nuts and seeds to add to their diet. It was still meager fare for elveens who were hiking all day long, but no one complained.

Late one morning, Tika noticed a number of conduits leading away from the central Line. She was tempted to follow them, but decided to keep to their course. After a few hundred more yards, though, she glanced along the path of one of the side conduits and saw something surprising.

"What's that?" she said out loud. "There, in the trees."

The four elven dropped their ponies' reins and walked together into the edge of the forest. The trees were younger here, shorter and less dense. This was obviously newer growth. They came up to the structure Tika had spotted, and stopped.

It was a cottage! Or at least, what was left of a cottage. There was no roof and no doors or windows. Trees were growing up through the floor inside. The elveens went in, curiosity overcoming fear. They had never seen a ruin of a building in their entire lives. Every structure in the Village was maintained in excellent condition. If an occupant died without kin, which was rare indeed, the Council gave their cottage to members of another family whose home was overfull.

"The conduit comes in here?" asked Br'on in disbelief.

"Yes," said Tika, turning around. With half-closed eyes, she followed the Line of Power, avoiding holes in the floor, into a room at the back of the cottage. Br'on, Moog and M'raj went to explore the rest of the building.

When Tika found the cookstones, however, her Hex failed, no matter how hard she Sent it. Was she going to be without Magik for the rest of their journey?

Then it occurred to her to follow the conduit more carefully through the cottage. She went back to the front of the cottage, and followed the conduit as it entered. She had assumed it would continue into the kitchen, but halfway through the cottage, her Sense of it disappeared.

Was it possible that *all* Power came from the Lines of Power rather than from Magik? Suddenly she remembered once last year, when Magik had failed completely in one of the cottages in the Village. At first, everyone thought the elven who lived there were to blame, but then they proved they could still heat cookstones in other elven's homes. Eventually, the Council had declared the cottage Dead, and the elven family had moved in with relatives. The 'dead' cottage had been turned into a storage shed, and, frightened that their own homes might be next, no one had mentioned it since, which is why she'd forgotten it until now.

Despite Tika's worry about the loss of her Magik, she tried to sound cheerful when she reported to the others. "It's too soon to quit for the day, but how about staying here for lunch?" she suggested. "Should be easier than trying to start a fire outside, wouldn't you say, Br'on?"

"I guess so," said Br'on. "I'll go get some food." His tone of voice said what he thought about eating a single boiled egg and some seed mash with berries, nuts and roots again. They had been carefully rationing the eggs, eating only one each, every two days, to make this valuable source of protein last as long as possible.

After they ate, they explored for a few more minutes, and then left. They recovered a couple of dishes they thought they could use, but no more food. One of the open cupboards had some large cylindrical metal containers in them, but they were too strange, so the elveens left them behind.

Calling their ponies, who had wandered off to graze, the foursome continued along the Line. When they saw another abandoned cottage, they were amazed. Then the number of cottages grew and grew, till they found themselves in another Village.

While Tika had been able to imagine another Village in a different Valley, it had never occurred to her there might be another Village in their own Valley. Especially an abandoned Village. For this entire Village was just like the cottage they'd found, with doors either hanging or gone, and trees growing up through floors.

It was eerie, thought Tika. On one hand, the shapes and sizes of some of the buildings were so familiar that she ached with homesickness. But other buildings looked to have been made of metal, though all that remained were the bare frames, like rusted skeletons reaching many stories into the sky. How could buildings ever have been so TALL?

Birds were nesting in the upper floors of the buildings, and squirrels and mice could be seen scampering in and out, the only signs of life. It was as if the Village itself had died. No elven, no laughter or shouting. No sounds of industry or play. No smell of bread baking. Her chest felt tight. What could have happened to the elven whose Village this was?

Along the sides of some of the streets were odd enclosed carts, such as a pony could pull, although they saw neither harness nor poles. Elfling stories included tales of 'ponyless carriages', Powered, one supposed, by Wizardelven far more powerful than the most powerful wizard in Elfdom. Br'on tried to open the door of one, but it was rusted closed, and he quickly gave up.

None of them spoke, though Tika was sure the others must be feeling the same way she was. There was something oppressive about the place. She wished they could just leave, but the Line went straight through the Village. She could sense conduits running into the buildings, and realized they could stay overnight in one of these buildings if they wanted to. She wasn't sure she did.

At last, as it was growing dark, they came to the far end of the Village. They couldn't help feeling relieved to be away from all of those ghosts of homes and metal skeletons. As they were passing one of the last ones, however, Tika felt compelled to suggest they try to see if its cookstones were still working. The other elveens agreed and the four cautiously entered.

After exploring for a few minutes, Tika gave a shout. "Come in here!" she called. "There's a cookstone in here that I can make work!"

She glanced at the ceiling, and sent the Lights Hex. Nothing happened. Oh, well …

M'raj was the first to arrive. "Wow!" she said. "That's definitely weird. The Power works, but the elven left. Why?"

"I think we should stay here for the night," said Tika, more relieved than she could say that at least some of her Magik seemed to be working once more. She had no sense of Net, though.

She realized suddenly that it had been days since she had even thought about Net! While growing up, Net had been a familiar friend in her head, a smart guide and teacher that was constantly with her. When she'd lost it in the Fair'day cave, she had felt like she would die. But here she was, living quite well without it!

The other three elveens somewhat reluctantly agreed to stay. It was definitely eerie to stay in the ghost of someone's cottage! But Br'on had discovered a tub full of rainwater out behind the cottage, and they led their ponies there, unloaded and rubbed them down, and let them drink.

The elveens were grateful, in the end, for the ease in cooking their meal, even if it was just more nuts and roots – it was a non-egg day. While Tika and Br'on made a passable soup, something they had all missed from home, Moog searched for tools he could take with them and M'raj fashioned waterbags from some of the waterproof containers they found in the cottage. These she filled, and then figured out to strap them onto the ponies' backs so they could take water with them when they left this place.

After some discussion, they decided to sleep inside, despite the spooky sensation of sleeping in someone else's cottage. It had been a long day. It was a very quiet evening. They couldn't stop wondering what had happened to the original elven from this Village. There was no precedent in their understanding that would help them to make sense of how it had ended up like this. Sleep was a long time coming.

When it was Tika's turn to take watch, she was really nervous. For some reason, being in a place where Magik was once more working made her afraid that Xinar would attack. She couldn't help wondering where he was – if he was standing in the shadows, observing her. The hairs on the back of her neck stood on end, but she didn't feel a MindTouch or see or hear anything that made her think her feeling was anything but anxiety.

She had no problem staying awake, though. Even after her four hours were up and she woke M'raj to take her turn, she tossed and turned in her blanket, unable to sleep.

The next morning, the Line out of the deserted Village led farther up the mountains, and Tika was afraid this meant they might be leaving the Valley entirely. Strangely, though, the path the Line followed had fewer trees than the forest on either side, and the stones beneath their feet were all flat on top. This suggested to Tika there had once been a street or road here, though she could see no reason for one, since the cottages and smaller conduits had stopped.

They continued to climb steadily for several days. It was easier walking on the stone road than in either the meadows or the forest, but the incline made their thigh muscles ache in ways they hadn't since the first few days of their trek. When they stopped one night, weary and discouraged, Br'on had bad news for them. "You know how sick we are of eggs? Well, now we're out of eggs."

"Great," sighed Moog, sitting on a fallen tree. "What are we going to eat?"

"I think we should rest here until tomorrow, and I will find and hunt an animal for us to eat," said Br'on.

"With what?" asked Tika, for aside from the eating knives every elf carried with them always, elven folk had no weapons.

"I'll show you tomorrow," said Br'on, exhausted. "I just want to sleep now."

When Tika awoke, hearing a noise, it was barely dawn. In the dim light, she could see Br'on busy near his pony. Quietly, so as not to wake M'raj or Moog, she untangled herself from her blanket and went to see what Br'on was doing.

From his saddlebag, he had taken his long knife and tucked it into his belt, so that it hung down his left leg. Despite his brown hair growing out raggedly, Br'on had fuzz beginning to sprout on his upper lip and chin. Tika realized that Br'on was starting to look more like an adult elf. It was strange, seeing her old enemy, now ally, look so mature.

As she approached, Br'on put a finger to his lips to indicate they shouldn't wake the others. Tika nodded, and then watched as Br'on took his stick with the string tied to one end and bent the wood by pushing against the ground with all his might. Then he attached the string to the other end, slipping a loop into a notch he had previously cut in the wood. When he let go, Tika was amazed to see the wood spring back, pulling the string taut.

"Neat," she whispered. "But what do you do with that, loop it around an animal's neck?"

Giving her a superior look, Br'on reached into his saddlebag and pulled out one of the shorter, thinner sticks with a pointed metal triangle strapped to one end. Tika noticed that the other end of the stick had feathers sticking out of some slits cut into it, with all but a small straight section of each feather cut off.

Glancing out of the corner of his eye to make sure she was watching, Br'on fit the feathered end of the stick onto the string, lining up with a notch cut apparently for that purpose. Then he held the wooden part of the string-thing in front of him with his left hand, and pulled the string and smaller stick back with the fingers of his right hand.

When he suddenly let go, the stick flew away so quickly Tika couldn't see it. It was as if it had disappeared. It reappeared a moment later, embedded in the trunk of a tree some twenty feet away.

"Wow!" said Tika, forgetting to whisper. "What kind of Hex is that?"

"Shhh," reminded Br'on, but it was too late, and soon he had M'raj and Moog for an audience as well.

"It's not a Hex at all. It's more like a tool," he explained. "This is called a bow," holding up the stick-and-string part, "and these are arrows. I shoot an arrow using the bow to make it go fast and hard, and if I can hit an animal with it, we'll eat meat tonight."

"Have you ever done that?" asked Moog, disbelief apparent on his face.

"I've done what's called target practice," responded Br'on. "That's shooting arrows at a specific spot, trying to get as close to the middle of the spot as possible."

"But you've never hunted an animal with an arrow?"

"Not yet. That's what I'm going to do today in this forest," said Br'on with more confidence than he really felt. "Speaking of which, Net said dawn and dusk were the best times to try to hunt animals. Apparently, they sleep in hiding most of the day. So I'd better be off." He turned to go.

"Can we come, too?" asked Tika, dying of curiosity to see how this new Hex would work. She couldn't quite believe the bow was a tool rather than a Hex.

"No," said Br'on fiercely. "Silence is necessary if I'm going to sneak up on an animal. Just take good care of Nu until I come back, okay?"

"Okay, I guess. Good luck," said Tika, trying to hide her disappointment. Then another thought occurred to her. "How will you know how to get back? Won't you get lost?"

Br'on looked blank. He obviously had not considered this problem. No one got lost in the Village, and since they'd begun their journey, they'd had the Line of Power to follow. He had no idea how to find his way back once he got out of sight.

Moog had an idea. "Wait a minute," he said. He went to his saddlebag, took out an empty food pouch, stooped and filled it with blossoms from a nearby shrub, and handed it to Br'on. "There," he said, "Luckily, there's no wind today. So, as you walk away, drop a blossom every ten steps or so. They're light enough in color to stand out against the needles on the ground. Then when you want to come back, follow the trail!"

"Good thinking, Moog!" said Br'on. "Thanks!"

Moog's ears glowed with embarrassment at the praise, and Tika thought once again that all of them had come a long way from their initial animosity. Then Br'on walked away into the woods, and there was little for the other three elveens to do except groom the ponies and try to brush the dirt off their own clothes. They didn't dare use any of their precious water to wash their clothes, for they had no idea how long it would be before they found another source.

When midday came and went, they ate some mushrooms Br'on had taught them were safe to eat, and then fell asleep beside their ponies, who were taking advantage of the break, and the soft ground to either side of the road, to lie down and rest.

Chapter Twenty: Br'on

It was late afternoon when they awoke. Br'on had not yet returned. "How long does it take to hunt a small animal?" asked Tika. "And didn't Br'on say only dawn and dusk were good for looking? Shouldn't he have been back by now?" She was really worried. She tried to Call him, but got no answer. *He must be too far away,* she thought. *Or my Hexes aren't working again.*

"Maybe we should follow the trail and find him," she said out loud. She didn't say out loud that maybe Xinar had attacked him, but she couldn't help thinking it!

"Well, it's nearly dusk now," said Moog. "If he wasn't successful this morning, maybe he didn't want to come back until he'd tried again. I don't think we should interrupt him if he's in the middle of hunting something. If he's not back tonight, we can go look for him tomorrow."

Br'on didn't return, though, and none of them slept much that night. What could have happened to him?

At dawn the next day, they were ready to go. They took all four ponies and began to follow the trail of blossoms. Luckily, these were easy to see, even in the dim light. They walked and walked without finding Br'on, however. They did cross a small creek, and stopped for a quick drink and to reload the water containers.

The sun was high overhead when they finally saw him, sitting with his back against a tree. Tika was instantly angry. How could he have been so rude to keep them waiting, while he just sat there? But as she got closer, she saw that his eyes were closed and his pant leg was red. She started to run, but M'raj, with her longer legs, quickly shot past her.

"Br'on!" M'raj screamed.

When they reached him, they saw that Br'on was badly hurt. The lower part of his pant leg was bloody, and there was a pool of blood under him. His face was too pale, and his breathing seemed shallow. When Tika touched his cheek, it was hot and clammy.

His eyes fluttered, and then opened. She could see he was in a lot of pain. "Oh, ha, Tika. I – think I'm hurt." Then his eyes closed again.

Tika glanced around, trying to understand what had happened to him. Beside him, his bow lay broken. There were no arrows to be seen. His left hand still held his sword. The edge was bloodied. So it seemed whatever had hurt him had been hurt as well.

Tika glanced at M'raj, horrified. M'raj reached down and ripped Br'on's pantleg so they could see the injury. Four parallel gashes ran down his calf, oozing blood. Tika felt ill. They needed a Healer! Then she reminded herself of the Healings she had done, and told M'raj to wash the cuts with clean water.

After that was done, she knelt beside Br'on, closed her eyes, and tried to use the skills she'd learned from her experiences with Wyryn. She pictured herself getting closer and closer to the cuts. Nothing happened. It was just her imagination—not at all like the Healings she'd done back in the Village.

. . . Back in the Village. *Yes!* She thought, *I need the Line of Power.* She stood up, and explained to the others. M'raj was a step ahead of her. She had pulled one of her spare shirts from her saddlebag and ripped it into strips with the help of her knife, and used the strips to bind the cuts, trying to stop the bleeding.

"He can't ride," said Moog, looking from Nu to Br'on. "Hang on! I remember something from our History class. He ran off into the woods and returned with two pine boughs. "Br'on always has rope in his saddlebags, so I'm going to try to make something called a travois," he said.

"Oh, like a cart without wheels," said M'raj. "Good idea! We can use his blanket to tie the branches together."

"Oh! And use the rope to attach the tra-vois to his pony," said Tika, stumbling over the unfamiliar word. Now she was sorry that she had never paid much attention in History class.

The three elveens worked quickly to build the travois, and then gently lifted Br'on onto it.

"It's going to be a bit bumpy," M'raj said, looking back at the way they had come.

"He's out of it," said Tika. "Let's just hurry."

Moog said nothing as Tika packed the broken bow and Br'on's 'knife' back into his saddlebag. Then they began to go back the way they came.

Once, Br'on opened his eyes and said simply, "Drink". They sat him up, put the waterbag to his lips, and he swallowed a sip or two, before falling back onto the sling once more.

"We should hurry," said Tika, although they were already walking quickly. Even after they broke into a trot, it seemed to take forever until they were back at the place they had stopped the previous day.

"Put him down here," said Tika, indicating a spot directly over the Line. Not wanting him to suffer even more, she put her hand on his forehead and sent Sleep.

Then she removed his bandages, washed the cuts with more clean water, and closed her eyes. This time, she was easily able to place her Mindself at the cuts, and See what needed to be done. First she stopped the bleeding, and then directed the white blobs (*did they have a real name?* she wondered for a second) toward the edges of the cut.

After a few minutes of concentration, something that looked like a bridge began to build over the open wounds, and she could sense new skin growing beneath the bridge. She directed the blobs to mend the muscle tissues beneath the skin as well, and to hunt down and destroy the infection that was giving Br'on a fever.

When she was done, the cuts were just puckered pink lines on his skin, though he kept dozing even after Tika Woke him. For the next few hours, Moog kept forcing Br'on to sip water and finally, as Sun was dropping in the west, his fever broke, and he was able to sleep naturally. M'raj built up the fire, while Tika covered Br'on with his blanket, and mentally checked his wounds from time to time.

Moog, M'raj and Tika were exhausted and frightened. Br'on hadn't regained consciousness enough to tell them what had happened to him. He had lost a lot of blood, and Tika had no idea how to tell his body to make more. She hoped all the water they gave him would help, but she felt horrible. *Why, oh why, had she led these elveens on this ridiculous Quest?*

Sleep was a long time coming, and filled with bad dreams. Tika was grateful to be shaken gently awake just after dawn. It was M'raj, crouched near her. "Br'on's awake, Tika."

She was on her feet instantly, running to his side. With Moog's help, he was sitting up, sipping water from a cup. He smiled weakly at Tika and M'raj.

"I guess I'm not as a good hunter as I thought," he said.

"What happened?" Tika asked, then added, "Are you strong enough to talk, or should you rest some more?"

"I can talk, but maybe no dancing today," said Br'on, winking with some of his old bravado. He closed his eyes and was silent for a few minutes, and they wondered if he'd gone back to sleep, but then he opened them again and sighed.

"Well, it went pretty well at first," he explained. "Net had told me to start at a source of water, because all animals need to drink. I guess you saw the stream I found. I waited and waited there, but no animals came to drink. I think maybe they could smell me there, or something." He stopped for another sip of water, but when Tika tried to tell him to rest and tell the story later, he waved her off.

"I'm okay," he said, glancing down at his leg, which was bandaged for several inches. "Thanks to you, I assume. Thanks for saving my life. I guess I would have bled to death if you hadn't found me."

He was silent for a moment. Then he stared at Tika, his eyebrows lifting almost to his hairline. "Hey! I didn't know you were such an Advanced Healer! How did you manage to learn that in your one week of Apprenticeship?"

Tika blushed. "Um … I just sort of accidentally found out how Healing works, and, yeah, so that's what I did." She glanced at the ground. "After we got you back to the Line, of course."

"What?" said Moog. "Nobody taught you? I thought one of the Healers must have been training you privately!"

"Nope. I figured it out for myself." She thought about trying to explain the Dark Pieces and the ladders inside the blobs, but decided not to risk their scorn when they didn't believe her. "I'm just glad it worked," she said, putting a hand on Br'on's shoulder. "It's my fault that you were injured."

"What? Don't be stupid, Tika. I was the one who decided to come, and I was the one who decided that I was the Great Hunter, ready to take on wild beasts. It's not your fault that I actually am stupid."

"Shut up, both of you!" cried M'raj. "Let's agree that we are all here of our own free choice, and no one is to blame when things go wrong. What's an Adventure without a little Danger, eh?"

She turned to Br'on. "So, are you up to telling us the rest?"

"Okay," he said, closing his eyes to pick up his train of thought, "So. After sitting beside the stream till dawn was long past, I finally saw a set of tracks. I didn't really know what animal they were from, but they were small, so that seemed like a good start. The ground was soft under the trees near the stream, so the tracks were fairly easy to follow.

"I was going as quietly as I could. . . . Finally I saw, in a small clearing ahead of me, a rabbit. You won't believe it, but I pulled my bow string, and killed it with my first shot! I was quite proud of myself!" Then Br'on fell silent, and Tika and M'raj wondered if they should let him sleep again.

"Do you want to lie down, Br'on?" asked Moog, who had been holding him upright.

"No, no, it's not that. . . . Okay, well. . . . Anyway, I went over to the rabbit and pulled the arrow out of it. That's when I heard this growling from behind me. I still had my bow in my hand, or I guess I'd be dead right now.

"There was this large cat-beast, light brown with a black and white muzzle, staring at me. It was bigger than me, and it was getting ready to pounce. As it jumped at me, I swung the bow at it like a club. The bow broke, but it prevented the beast from landing on top of me. Then I pulled out my sword and prepared to fight.

"The cat charged at me again, and I think I hit it with the sword, but it slashed me with its claws, and I fell back against the tree. I thought I was dead for sure. I felt weak and dizzy, and was sure if it jumped at me again, I wouldn't be able to defend myself.

"But all it did was slink up to the rabbit, pick it up in its mouth and run away." Br'on smiled wryly. "All it wanted was the rabbit. If I had just stepped away from the rabbit in the first place, it might never have attacked me. It just never occurred to me, guys. It just never occurred to me."

"Don't worry about it, Br'on. We're just glad you're okay. Who needs meat, anyway?" M'raj's smile was reassuring. "But gosh, Br'on, I thought goof-ups were Moog's department!"

All of the elveens laughed, and the tension of the moment broke. It was three days before Br'on was able to use his leg again, and even then he limped for a long time. Still, he insisted they continue their journey. His saddlebags were split between the other ponies since they made him ride Nu. He taught them how to collect seeds from pine cones trees, and how to recognize more mushrooms Net had said were not poisonous. "We won't starve, even without meat," he assured his friends.

He was ecstatic when he learned they had recovered his weapons. One evening, after he was once again able to walk, he hobbled about in search of a strong, pliable branch to replace the broken bow.

"Even if I don't hunt," he explained, "we could still use it for defense."

No one mentioned the danger from the big cat-beast, but they continued to take turns guarding and sleeping in shifts. There might be wild dogs in these mountains, too. No one mentioned Xinar or his apprentices.

When Br'on found a branch he liked, he and M'raj cut it off of the tree, and he showed her how to attach the string to one end, bend the bow, and attach the string to the other end, using notches to prevent the string from sliding down the branch. Of course, this made M'raj want her own bow, and Tika and Moog did, too. Luckily, Br'on had brought lots of extra string, and could show them how to make arrows out of straight branches (without the metal tips or feathers, unfortunately), but soon all four elveens were spending their evenings in target practice.

The first time Moog tried to pull the string back, though, he was amazed how hard it was to do. The bent branch made the string very tight, and it didn't want to be pulled, it seemed. Br'on had made it look easy, and Moog didn't want to look like a weakling, so he pulled with all his might.

When he had the string back at his ear, though, as Br'on had taught him, the bow slipped out of his left hand and smacked him in the face, knocking him onto his back.

M'raj, Br'on and Tika burst into laughter. Moog sat rubbing the goose-egg on his forehead, grinning foolishly, and wondering if he would ever learn to be useful. In fact, all four elven had two other problems with their new weapons. The first was that they couldn't make the arrows fly straight, and the second was that the green twigs they were using simply bounced off the tree trunks they used as targets.

When they found a dead bird one day, Br'on pulled a handful of feathers from the stiff carcass, and that night, he showed the others how to cut slots into the string-end of the arrows. Then he cut the feathers quite close to the shaft, and slid the shaft of a feather into each slot. "This helps the arrow fly straight toward the target," he explained. "That and a lot of practice." He smiled at their clumsiness as they learned.

"It's too bad we lost the metal-tipped arrows," said M'raj as they shot their newly-feathered arrows at the cloth target Br'on had hung on a tree. "The tips of these are too soft to hunt anything."

"Dry wood is harder than wet, isn't it?" asked Tika.

"Yes," agreed Br'on, "but the dead twigs on the ground are so brittle they shatter as soon as they hit something."

"Okay, so what if we dry out the ends of these sticks over the fire?" suggested Tika. "If we can prevent them from catching fire, wouldn't they get at least somewhat harder?"

"Well, Net suggested that with the sword. I put it in the fire, then banged the edge sharp with a hammer, then put it in cold water to cool it, over and over again. Net called this 'tempering' the metal," said Br'on.

"I don't think the cold water part would be a good idea. The wood would just absorb it, but the heat thing might work. We could just lay them on the hot rocks around the fire," put in M'raj.

So the four friends took their arrows and hardened the tips by letting them bake on the rocks. Sure enough, the next time they tried them, their arrows sank into the trunk of the tree rather than bouncing off.

There was no metal around to make them swords of their own, but Moog, Tika and M'raj took to carrying their eating knives in their belt as Br'on wore his sword.

"Now we're ready for anything," said Tika proudly, little realizing how quickly – and surprisingly – she would be proved wrong.

Chapter Twenty-One: the Robot

It seemed they had been climbing forever, and yet whenever they reached a clearing, they could see the mountain stretching endlessly up in front of them. Just when Tika began to feel they were never going to stop walking, however, the landscape began to change subtly.

Early one morning, they reached another plateau, a large grassy plain halfway up the side of the mountain. Here the Line of Power once again sprouted conduits, so many of them Tika could hardly believe her Senses. Yet looking around, she could see no cottages or other buildings, abandoned or not. Just muted green and golden grasses that signaled the coming of fall, rippling gently like the surface of the lake in a wind.

Continuing to follow the Line, Tika noticed black posts among the nearest trees which edged the plain. One of the conduits she could sense obviously ran toward a post, and she turned to follow it. As they approached the post, a voice rang out, though there was no one to be seen.

The voice made a number of sounds, all garbled, but sounding something like words which they couldn't understand. Finally, they heard it say, "Stop. Restricted area. Authorized personnel only. Identify!" The accent was strange, and sounded like ancient Elvish.

The four elven looked at each other, and then dismounted and turned quickly so their backs were together in a tight square, as Br'on had taught them for defense. Br'on was determined no one should ever surprise him from behind as the cat had done, and so the four companions had practiced this defensive posture, guarding each other's backs.

There didn't seem to be anyone around. Nevertheless, Tika found the hairs on her neck and arms standing on end. Something wasn't right. She mentally Called a greeting, but no one answered.

Tika stepped close to the post. "Greetings," she said quietly. "I am Wizardelf Tika Tamir, Elf One of the D'inn-Tiriki-K'ah-Ch'anja parentgroup. I have Sup'rvis Authorization, Access Code Tika 97114B4. Who are you?"

The voice repeated its warning until Tika, exasperated, Sent "Oh, will you Shut Up!" The voice was silenced. She looked at the post again, and walked closer to it. There was a flat piece of metal attached to the post, with a number of straight and curved lines etched onto it. It made no sense to Tika.

"Let's go back and follow the main Line," she suggested. She didn't mention that at least Xinar couldn't lurk in the shadows, once they were out on the open plain. She realized she would soon feel safer than she had in weeks.

As they crossed the plain, continuing to lead their ponies along the ancient road, they could see a broad flat cliff face on the far side, with a dark semi-circle in the middle that looked like a cave. The Line was heading right toward it.

She looked at the other elveens. "Do you want to go on?" she asked. "We don't know what's ahead, but elven must have lived here once, don't you think?"

The other elveens looked at each other and nodded, then pulled their bows from their saddlebags and strung arrows. Tika placed her hand on her knife, and the foursome started forward.

Suddenly, from the mouth of the cave burst a monster. Elflings all hear stories of supernatural beings, monsters with glowing eyes and thirty arms who eat elflings for breakfast. This monster seemed to have no arms at all, but possessed eyes which glowed in a line right across its 'head'. It was no taller than the elveens, but they were terrified nonetheless.

They must have communicated their fear to their ponies, for they began to snort and paw the ground. Tika could see the whites of Blaize's eyes, and knew the pony was close to bolting.

She was ready to turn and run, but Br'on stopped her by reaching over to place a warm hand on her arm. "When will we be better prepared than now?" he asked simply, putting down his bow and taking his sword into his hand. "Does the Line not lead into that cave? I say, we fight the monster. Let the ponies go. They won't go far."

Moog, Tika and M'raj obeyed. They didn't have time to worry about the ponies because the monster was approaching rapidly. Tika could see that Moog was trembling, just as she was, but they stood their ground. M'raj looked more excited than afraid.

The monster stopped a few yards from them. It hovered a foot or so above the grasses, which churned beneath it as if in a storm. To Tika, its shape was like a finger-tip – a tube with a rounded top. As they had seen from farther off, it had no arms or legs, just the single row of glowing red eyes that appeared to go all the way around its body. The eyes blinked at different rates, and Tika wasn't sure where to direct her focus.

Then it spoke, speaking garbled sounds, pausing, then more garbled sounds, until it said something they could recognize. "Stop. Top Secret. Restricted area. Authorized personnel only. Identify!"

Top Secret! That's what Proxy had said! This must be the right place! So Tika Sent, "I am Wizardelf Tika Tamir, Elf One of the D'inn-Tiriki-K'ah-Ch'anja parentgroup. I have Sup'rvis Authorization, Access Code Tika 97114B4. Who are you?" She waited to see if her Hex had worked.

The monster's eyes blinked rapidly, as if it was thinking. Then it said, "Authorization not recognized. Leave here at once!"

Before Tika could respond, she saw an arrow fly from M'raj's bow. It struck one of the lights, and shattered it. With a roar, Br'on limped forward as fast as he could, and grabbing her knife, Tika followed. Moog was right beside her, knife in hand.

"Authorization . . ." began the monster once more, and then the four elveens were on it. Moog slashed at it with his knife. Br'on drove his sword through another eye, and Tika and M'raj stabbed it with their knives.

After a few tense moments, the monster dropped to the ground and went silent, the glow fading from its eyes. They pulled their weapons out, and jumped back, ready to attack again.

But the monster appeared dead. With a jerk of his head, Br'on indicated they should approach the beast. When they were right next to it, Tika put her knife back in her belt. While the others stood ready, she Sent, "Greetings." There was no response. The monster was silent. She reached out a shaky hand and touched its skin. It was cold. She looked closer.

"Its skin is metal!" she declared. "Br'on, Moog, M'raj, feel it!"

Keeping their weapons ready, the other elveens touched the monster's skin.

"I think you're right," said Moog. "It looks and feels like metal … Could it be a tool? Elven-made?"

This reminded Tika of her theory about the Dark Pieces and the Lines of Power being not natural, and she began to see a pattern. "I think it *is* elven-made," she said. "Just like the Lines of Power, and the Dark Pieces inside us that we can direct to heal one another."

"No elf that I know could have made a monster – or a tool – like this," said Moog, running his hand along the skin of the thing. "And if the broken and overgrown fence is any indication, it must have been made a very long time ago. Did elven use to know more than we do now?"

It was a strange and disturbing thought. Tika was a bit sorry they had killed the monster. Perhaps it could have told them more. But no, it had insisted they leave, and that was one thing they could not do. They had had no choice, just as they now had to face going into the cave. Fortunately, just as Br'on had predicted, the ponies had run a few hundred yards and then stopped, so it was easy to Call them back.

"I don't think we should take the ponies in," Tika told the others as they started forward again. "We need to find them some water. There's plenty to eat here, and they won't go far. We'll take off the saddlebags, and then let them go." She didn't mention the possibility that they might not return from the cave.

"I'm going to take this monster-tool with us," Moog announced. "Maybe I can fix it … Br'on, could you help me load it onto Mooky? I'll get him to carry it to the cave, and then see what we can do with it there."

Shrugging, Br'on did as Moog had asked, and a few minutes later, the elveens had led their ponies to the mouth of the cave, where they removed the saddlebags and halters from the ponies.

"We should get fresh water for ourselves, too," suggested M'raj. "We could refill our waterbags to carry with us into the cave." The others agreed, and they pulled out the empty waterbags and took them along. As they turned and walked away, the ponies followed obediently. Br'on had spotted something glittering against the mountain face off to their right, and sure enough, a small waterfall cascaded through a crevasse in the side of the cliff into a small stream.

"This looks just right," said Tika, trying to sound cheerful, when in fact she felt like crying. She was afraid she would never see her beloved Blaize again. She knew her pony could survive out here, with plenty to eat and drink, but would she herself survive the cave?

If the other three elveens felt the same way, they tried not to show it. All four gave their ponies a good rubbing down and a friendly scratch. Then they filled their waterbags, turned and walked away. When it seemed the ponies would follow, they told them, "Stay!" They walked away, forcing themselves not to look back, for all four were fighting tears. Suddenly, the dangers and troubles they had faced up to now seemed easy in comparison.

Chapter Twenty-Two: the Cave

A few minutes later, they were back at the cave. Up close, they could see that the mouth of the cave wasn't natural. Some kind of gray dirt had been tightly packed into an arc that ran up the sides and across floor of the cave, making it look more like a giant room than a cave. They saw the remains of another fence, and then noticed there were doors built into the cave walls.

Weapons in hand, the four advanced toward one of the pale green doors, which were even taller than the tallest door in Elfdom. Br'on placed a hand lightly against it.

"It's made of metal!" he exclaimed. "No one in the Smelter's Guild could Shape a piece of metal this huge!"

When he tried the door handle, though, it wouldn't budge. He glanced at Tika wordlessly. She Sent a Command for it to open. Br'on tried it again. Still nothing. M'raj and Moog tried their Hexes. Nothing.

"It's not along the main Line of Power anyway," said Tika. "That goes straight back." Straight back into utter darkness. "Um, . . . maybe we should eat first, and then pack some supplies to take with us."

They went back to their saddlebags, and removed some of the mushrooms, nuts and roots they had gathered along the way. They drank the fresh water gratefully.

"The saddlebags are too heavy for us to carry," said Br'on. "We need something smaller.

"How about our blankets?" said Tika. "That way, we'll have our blankets and our food."

"Good thinking," said Moog, immediately setting to work opening up his blanket and loading far too much food into it. Tika smiled at M'raj as they watched, but neither said a word. They had long since stopped teasing Moog about his appetite, for he did more than his share of food-gathering.

"What about the monster?" M'raj asked Moog. "It's too heavy for us to carry."

Moog's face fell. "I guess we'll have to leave it behind," he said. "I only brought my most basic tools with me, anyway."

"What are we going to do for light?" asked Br'on.

"Couldn't we just Send a Hex?" said M'raj.

"I could try," smiled Tika, and closed her eyes. "Lights!" she Sent. Even with her eyes still closed, she could tell her Hex had worked. But nothing could have prepared her for what she saw when she opened them.

The cave was lit with brilliant lights, more lights than she had ever seen! They ran in a straight line along the center of the ceiling. She had to blink a couple of times to adjust to the brightness. Then she saw that the 'cave' went back inside the mountain as far as she could see, and probably farther!

She looked at her friends. They, too, were staring down the long, long corridor in amazement.

Suddenly, Tika became aware of Net in her mind like a distant voice. Net!! She gasped. It was like a relative had returned from the grave!

"What's the matter, Tika!" asked M'raj, looking concerned. "You just went pale all of a sudden."

"I – uh –" Tika's lifelong secret was stuck in her throat. But after all they'd been through, surely it was time to confess?

"Are you okay?" asked Moog.

"What's going on?" asked Br'on.

"Um … Okay. Maybe we should sit down for a moment."

The other elveens sat down, their faces full of the questions they weren't asking.

After a moment, Tika cleared her throat and tried again. "Um … You know how you – I mean, we – Access Net at CenOps?"

Everyone nodded, looking puzzled.

"Well, um … I actually don't need CenOps, or a Vee'ar helmet, to Access Net … I just – sort of – hear it inside my head."

All three elveens jumped to their feet and started talking at the same time. Tika put her hands over her ears. "QUIET!" she begged.

After a moment, the others settled back down.

"Is this true? Why didn't you – EVER – tell me?" M'raj asked, looking hurt. "Don't you trust me?"

"Oh, M'raj, this is exactly why I didn't tell ANYONE – not even my parentgroup – that I have this ability … When I was little, I just assumed everyone could do it. But when I asked questions, elven just told me to go to CenOps to get my answers. So – I figured out that nobody but me had this ability. I was scared to tell anyone. I was already being bullied for being different …" Tika was careful not to look at Br'on, but the other two did, which told Tika that they knew he'd been part of the group that had bullied her.

"So why did you – why were you always in CenOps?" M'raj asked. "I mean, if you don't need a Vee'ar helmet, why put one on?"

"Oh. That. Well, it's much easier for me to Access Net in CenOps. Like a close voice instead of a far-away voice … As for the helmet, I would have looked very strange in CenOps without one, right? … I'm sorry, M'raj. I should have trusted you not to freak out. But you were my first friend – my ONLY friend – and I didn't want to take the chance that you wouldn't want to be my friend if you knew – what a freak I REALLY am."

M'raj came over and pulled Tika to her feet, enveloping her in a hug. "I love you, you weirdo," she said. "Thanks for telling us."

Tika turned to the other elveens to see how they were taking the news.

"So how come you haven't solved the Power issue before now?" said Moog, his voice a bit sad.

"I don't have Authorization to Access the information," said Tika. It's not about how or where you ask, it's about Authorization."

"So – what can you tell us about this place?" asked Br'on. "Access Net and find out."

Tika closed her eyes, trying to make sense of the babble of Net. After a moment, she opened them again. "I – can't. At least, not yet. I am aware of Net, but when I Send a Query, there's no answer … I don't know why."

"Yeah, what *is* this place?" whispered M'raj.

"You mean, what *was* this place," corrected Br'on, pointing. Along the far side of the cave were many strange, open carriages, like those they'd seen in the abandoned Village, covered with a thick coat of dust.

After eating and drinking, the four elveens settled their blanket-burdens crosswise across their backs and walked toward the carriages. Tika noted it took a couple of hundred steps to walk the width of the cave. *Elven had made this? How could they? And what for?* Each new discovery only seemed to lead to more and more questions. She began to wonder if they would ever find the Source, and if they did, whether they would be able to understand it well enough to fix it. She sighed, and brought her attention back to the present. One problem at a time.

Up close, Tika realized gratefully that the carriages were smaller than the ones in the abandoned Village – closer to elf-sized. They had no top, which made sense, if they were used inside a cave where weather would never be a concern. There were four seats in each one, and a stick with a kind of round wheel-thing on top in front of one seat.

"How would you hook a pony to this thing?" asked Tika, thinking how nice it would be go have Blaize along. "It would sure be nice not to have to walk all the way through a mountain." She smiled at the others.

"Maybe it doesn't need a pony," said Moog, thinking out loud. "The monster-tool we killed outside wasn't pulled by a pony, or even walk."

They were all silent for a moment, remembering. At the time, they hadn't been too surprised that a 'monster' could float toward them, hovering a foot or so above the grass. But even when the monster turned out to be a tool rather than a beast, no one had had time to wonder how it traveled.

Br'on reached out and touched the smooth, pale surface of the carriage. "It's not made of metal," he said. "It's not as cold – more like wood would be, except it doesn't look like any wood I've ever seen." He put down his blanket-bag and began to brush centuries' worth of dust off of the thing, sending them all into fits of coughing. But finally, he had uncovered enough for them to have a better look.

"It does sort of resemble the monster-tool," said M'raj, examining the carriage thoughtfully. "Those things there look like its eyes after we killed it and they went dull. – Only I guess they weren't 'eyes'. What were they?"

"Tiny lights!" exclaimed Moog, suddenly knowing. "We're used to lights in our ceilings, like those above us here. But there's no reason lights couldn't be smaller, and put into a tool for some reason. Right?"

"Hey, if the lights here responded to a Hex, maybe this carriage would, too," said Br'on. "It's sure worth a try. Tika?"

Tika looked at him. "What kind of Hex should I use?" she asked. "I can't just say 'Lights' or this would already be working."

"Hmmm," said Moog. "How about Go?" He had closed his eyes as he said it, and didn't see as the carriage lifted off of the ground and began to move forward, nearly knocking Br'on down.

"Hey!" yelled Br'on. "Stop!"

"Sorry," said Moog, smiling sheepishly. "I didn't actually mean to Send."

The carriage must have been very sensitive to Hex, thought Tika, because Br'on had made it come to a stop. It settled back down to the ground, several yards away. "Good Hexing, guys," she smiled. "I don't think we're going to need a pony."

Excited for the first time since they'd mastered their bows and arrows, the four elveens climbed into the carriage. They piled their blankets and waterbags in the space behind the back seats.

Br'on suggested Tika should sit in the seat with the wheel-stick. "That looks like the main seat," he said. "And you're the one who's following the Line."

She sat in the seat. It seemed natural to rest her hands on the wheel-thing. Once the other three were settled in, she Sent the Hex, "Go!" as Moog had, and once again, the carriage rose gently into the air and began to move forward. *The balance was a little off,* Tika thought, and leaned to the right, unconsciously turning the wheel beneath her hands. The carriage turned in the same direction and began to head for the wall of the cave.

"Stop!" she Sent in a panic, and was relieved when the carriage settled to the ground.

"What happened?" asked Moog, wishing he could have taken that seat. The carriage had gone straight when *he* was controlling it. If it was a tool, then maybe someone from the Fixit Guild should guide it!

"I don't know," said Tika, thinking back. "I felt a bit off-balance, and then I shifted sideways, and the wheel turned, and the next thing I knew we were here."

"It must be that wheel-thing has something to do with direction, like pulling the reins on a pony," said Moog. "Why don't you try it again? This time, turn the wheel the other way, and see if we head back down the cave?"

So up they went again, and after making everyone laugh by turning them around first one way, then the other, Tika got the hang of controlling the wheel with small motions, and they began heading down the cave. It was much easier than walking but she wasn't sure she wanted to find out what was at the other end.

Chapter Twenty-Three: Access Denied

The corridor was very long and it was obvious they were heading down as well as forward. That was scary. All elflings hear stories of Trolls who live under the ground, and although the four elveens could laugh at this now, there was enough elfling left in each of them for the hairs on their arms and necks to stand on end. They kept glancing around fearfully, but saw nothing but smooth, arced walls and closed doors.

Finally, they saw something different. A curved line of blue lights followed the arc of the walls and ceiling overhead. As they passed beneath this, there was a small beep from the front of the carriage, and a small female materialized on a flat panel at the front of the carriage.

This time, there was no babbling. "Welcome to the Central Intelligence Bunker, or See-Eye, as we call it," said the tiny creature in funny-sounding Elvish. Tika, M'raj, and Br'on all stared at her in amazement. Although female-looking, it was obvious she was not elven. Instead of having long, mobile, double-tipped ears, useful and graceful, the ears of this poor deformed creature were mere semi-circular knobs of flesh sticking out the sides of her head, unmoving. How horrible! And she stood only half as tall as even a short elf like Tika. Worse, her tiny eyes were so close together on the front of her face that she would have embarrassed her parentgroup. Who *was* she?

"Greetings," said Tika bravely. "I am Wizardelf Tika Tamir, Elf One of the D'inn-Tiriki-K'ah-Ch'anja parentgroup. Who are you?"

It was as if the small creature were deaf, for she continued to speak as if Tika had not said a thing. "See-Eye is the largest fully-automated Knowledge Collection and Storage facility in the world. In addition, we are the central monitoring system for Solar Energy Collection and Weather Control on Space Station Hawking, named for Ethan, the great-grandson of the twentieth-century genius, Stephen Hawking."

She was speaking the same strange dialect of Elvish as had the monster and the post, and the four elveens had trouble understanding her. She was also using words they had never heard of. What did 'automated' mean?

Br'on pulled his sword out of his belt, and held it in front of the being. "Who are you? Identify yourself!" he demanded.

"The tunnel you are traveling through will take you continuously downhill from the mountain entrance," the creature was saying in a relentlessly-cheerful voice, "as the Bunker is located nearly six miles underground."

"Shut up!" said Br'on, getting angrier by the minute. Finally, he poked her gently with his sword to get her attention, but the sword went right through her without interrupting her speech!

"Yep. She's a holo," confirmed M'raj in wonderment. "But who's Sending her?"

"It must be the carriage," guessed Tika. "Maybe one of those buttons will quiet her." She pointed to a series of colored buttons in front of Br'on, each with sticks and squiggly lines underneath.

He pressed the first one on the left. The carriage immediately stopped, and floated gently to the ground. The female creature kept babbling, about such strange things as 'personnel' and 'strategic defense'.

"That wasn't the right button," Br'on said, and pressed the next one. Lights shone from the front of the carriage, illuminating the floor of the tunnel even more brightly than before. Br'on shrugged, and tried the next button. A brilliant beam of light shot out of the front of the car, and from a distance, they could see the flash of an explosion. All four elveens jumped, but the holo creature continued to jabber.

Br'on looked at M'raj and Tika, as if worried about what they might say. "Let's not use that one again soon," suggested Tika in a small voice.

There was one button left, and Br'on pushed it carefully, ready to jump out if the carriage caught fire. Fortunately, all that happened was the holo disappeared, and all everyone sighed with relief.

"What was that – creature?" Tika asked, making no attempt to get the carriage moving again. She wanted a minute to settle her nerves.

"Not elven, at any rate," said Br'on. "Did you see those *ears*?"

M'raj shuddered. "Not only were they deformed, they were *paralyzed*! How would anyone know what she was feeling?"

"And her pitiful little *eyes!* Maybe an accident at birth?" said Tika. "Not her fault, poor creature . . . so tiny!" She smiled. "And I thought *I* was short!"

All four elven laughed, and some of their tension passed.

"She called this cave a 'tunnel'," said M'raj. "I didn't understand a lot of the other words she said."

"Maybe an elf-made – or creature-made – cave is called a 'tunnel'," speculated Tika.

"Well, should we continue down our – tunnel?" Br'on asked, trying out the new word.

Tika and M'raj looked at each other, shrugged, and then Tika Sent, "Go!" to the carriage. It rose gently in the air and they were once more on their way. Not sure what lay ahead, they took advantage of the opportunity to eat and drink.

Chewing on a stale, rubbery tree mushroom, Moog made a face. "It sure would be nice to have some real food to eat one of these days," he said. "I'm starting to miss the eggs!" His gap-toothed grin was infectious, and the others smiled back in spite of their own anxieties.

It was tempting to stop and investigate some of the dozens of doors they passed, but the Line of Power led straight down the tunnel, and Tika felt they were close to their goal. The elveens grew increasingly nervous and afraid. They were a long, long way from the sunshine they had left behind! The tunnel seemed to go on forever, so it was with some relief that Br'on finally noticed something different in the distance.

"I think we're finally getting to end of the tunnel," he said.

The carriage settled gently to a stop in front of a set of massive doors. Looking at each other, not sure exactly what to do, they got carefully out of the carriage, stretching to relieve their cramped muscles. Upon closer inspection, Tika could tell the doors were made of metal. They were painted emerald green, and this far from sunlight, the color was still bright.

"Now what?" asked M'raj. "How are we going to get in?"

Glancing around, Tika nodded left. The four elveens went toward the booths she had spotted. The booths looked comfortingly familiar, almost the same as those in CenOps.

"I think we should each take a booth," suggested Tika. "That way, we can all try our luck."

"You don't really need one, though, do you?" M'raj asked.

"It's probably easier in the booth," Tika admitted, entering one.

The equipment in the booth wasn't as similar as Tika had thought it was. There was no Vee'ar helmet, simply a metal ring that looked like the circlets worn by some of the Wizardelven. Tika picked up the ring and slid it over her head. It was too large, but luckily, could be adjusted to fit, just like the helmets in CenOps at home. At first, nothing happened, and she removed the ring to inspect it again.

This time, she noticed there were squiggles like the elveens had seen in the carriage. Intuitively, Tika turned these toward the front, and slid the ring over her head again. Without any weight pressing on her ears, it was much more comfortable than the helmets in CenOps. But still nothing happened.

"Access Net," she Sent with her eyes closed. Immediately, she found herself in a holo, like no Vee'ar she'd been in before. She appeared to be in a windowless metal room. The walls gleamed faintly as if highly polished, though there was no light source to be seen. She was alone, and wondered how to proceed.

Then next thing she knew, though, Br'on appeared on one side of her, and Moog and M'raj on the other.

"Ha, guys," she said to her friends. "Welcome to . . . the metal room." She couldn't help smiling as she realized the others had made avatars of themselves far different than the dirty and bedraggled elveens who had entered the booths. Br'on's hair shone, and he was wearing a Wizardelf's robe. He looked noble, and she refrained from commenting that he had never been named Wizard. Moog, too, appeared in the garments of a Wizardelf, and his orange hair was also clean and neat. His skyblue eyes were gleaming with anticipation. M'raj wore her favorite orange tunic and her blue hair shone with ribbons.

Tika, to be fair, had also projected an image of herself from better days, too. In Net, her hair was still long, tied sedately with ribbon to hang down her back. Her skin, like Br'on's and M'raj's, was once again clean, and her lips not cracked and sunburned. None of them looked as thin as they had all become.

"I've never met another elf in Net before," commented Br'on. "Have any of you?"

The others shook their heads. "It's kind of nice," Tika said. "But now what?"

"Do you think Proxy is here?" asked M'raj.

"I guess I'll try to find out," said Tika. "Net, Query Proxy, guardian of Top Secret and Eyes Only Knowledge."

For a moment, it seemed as though Tika had not been heard, and then the large red dragon appeared in front of them.

"Tika Tamir, what a pleasant surprise to find you here," said Proxy smoothly. "I don't believe I know your companions?"

"This is Br'on Lleyn, this is M'raj Al'bani and this is Moog Moe'bis," answered Tika, leaving out their parentgroup names in her nervousness. "We seek Knowledge on the loss of Power within the Village."

When a huge, gleaming red dragon smiles, it is not a reassuring sight, Tika realized.

"We have followed the 'string' as you suggested, and it led here," she explained, talking to cover her fear. "This must be the Source of the Village's Power, but it leads behind the emerald doors. Can you let us in?"

"I wish I could," said Proxy, her red eyes looking sad, "but Access is for Authorized Personnel only, and you aren't on the list."

"I have Sup'rvis Authorization," insisted Tika, "and so do Moog and M'raj. Is that not enough?"

"Unfortunately, no," said Proxy.

"This is stupid!" said Br'on. "We have travelled for many days, across the entire Valley, and faced dangers and starvation. It was your stupid hint that led us here, and now you're telling us you're not going to let us in?"

"I can't," said Proxy. "I have no algorithm for doing so."

Br'on looked over at Tika, and said, "Let's get out of here for a minute. I think we should talk."

They exited the Vee'ar, and came out of the booths. It made Tika sad to see the others back in their torn, dirty clothes, but then she reached up and touched the end of her own closely-cut hair, and said nothing.

"Can we fight her?" said Br'on.

"How?" Tika asked.

"Well, we have weapons out here. Can't we imagine something in the Vee'ar that we could fight her with?"

"Like what?"

"Maybe a better bow," Br'on said. "With arrows that can pierce a dragon's hide."

"You've got a good imagination, Br'on," said M'raj, "but if Proxy is *part* of the Vee'ar, isn't she going to *know* what we're doing, and change herself to be always a step ahead of us?"

Br'on didn't answer for a moment. Then, sighing, he walked over to the carriage, and pulled out a waterbag. "I don't know about you two, but I'm thirsty, and tired. Maybe we should sleep on this."

"Maybe Proxy knows where we can at least get some food," said Moog. "I'm going back in to ask her."

He returned a few minutes later, his gap-toothed grin triumphant. "I talked Proxy into letting us into some place she called 'Media Quarters', where we can get food. We need to go in the carriage," he added, climbing into the seat with the wheel. "I'll direct. Proxy told me where to go."

Tika, M'raj and Br'on climbed in without argument, and Moog managed to turn the carriage around and head back up the tunnel. He took to Controlling the carriage much faster than she had, Tika realized. Maybe it was a Fixit skill? Just as they were beginning to wonder if he actually knew where he was going, Moog directed the carriage toward one of the doors they had passed previously.

Tika was just thinking how impressed she was with the way he had taken charge, when he miscalculated their stop, and the carriage hit the door and dropped to the ground like a rock. Tika in the back seat was thrown forward into Br'on, who banged his head on the carriage's frame. M'raj banged into Moog's back, and Moog would have been thrown out entirely had he not hit the steering wheel first.

"Oof!" he said, settling back down and looking sheepish. "Sorry about that. Just give me a second. I'll fix it." He concentrated, and the carriage rose in the air, backed off several feet, and settled to the ground again. "There, that's better. You okay?" he asked his friends.

Br'on was rubbing a goose-egg on his forehead. "Fine," he mumbled, trying to contain his temper. "So how do we get in the door?"

"Magik," smiled Moog. "Proxy gave me Authorization. Just watch." He walked up beside the door, and put his right eye very close to a box none of the other elveens had noticed. He held very still, and Tika wondered what he was staring at. Then a green light suddenly shone above the door, which slid open with a 'whoosh', raising a cloud of dust. Moog began to sneeze loudly, making him unable to speak, so he gestured them to enter.

Inside, the room was the opposite of the dusty corridor. Every surface shone as if someone had just cleaned it. It made Tika uneasy, as if, once again, they were walking into someone else's cottage while they were away.

Seeing the look on her face, Moog said reassuringly, "It's okay, Tika. I'm not sure what Proxy meant by 'Media', but I did get the idea that this place is–was?–intended for guests." He looked around. "Sure is clean, huh?"

The room was, in fact, totally white. White walls, floor, and ceiling. White tables and chairs. It was eerie, thought Tika. It made her feel as if there were something wrong with her eyes. Were the creatures who made this room afraid their guests might hate color?

Br'on was exploring. "So where's the food, Hollow Leg?"

Moog looked around, searching for something. "Um . . . Proxy said it looked like one of our oven doors . . . There!" He walked over to a wall, and pointed to a small door just about head-height. "Proxy said to speak our request, and then wait. She said the food here is frozen and dried, I think. Some of what she said didn't make much sense. I'm going to request chicken, I think." He walked up to the door and said, "Chicken!"

A disembodied voice responded, "Processing. One moment, please."

A minute or so later, the door went "Bing!" and Moog opened it. The dish he pulled out didn't look like chicken. More like soup. "Oh, yeah," he said, remembering. "Proxy said the only food left in storage is soup. Well, that's okay, I haven't had chicken soup in a long time." He took his dish and walked over to a table, which again was about shoulder height. He had to climb to get onto the chair.

"Looks like giants lived here, too," said Br'on, and then turning to Tika and M'raj, said, "You two next."

While M'raj told the food door her request, Tika hesitated, looking over at Moog. "Don't you need a spoon?" she asked him.

Moog had been busy fishing chunks of chicken out of the steaming dish with his fingers. "If you can find one," he mumbled around a mouthful of food. "This is good!"

Tika Queried, "Spoon!" and got a picture in her head of a drawer near the food door. She walked over. The wall appeared featureless at first, but when Tika looked carefully, she could see small indentations in the white surface. She reached out and put her finger into the space, thinking she would have to pull the drawer out. Instead, as soon as she touched it, the door slid toward her head! She jumped back. When it seemed the drawer had stopped moving, she walked forward again, trying to see into it. But she was too short.

She looked over her shoulder. "Um, M'raj, could you please?"

The taller elf looked into the drawer, and brought out four spoons, which thankfully were a comfortingly familiar shape and metal, not white. She handed one to Tika, and took the others to the table.

Tika turned her attention to the food door, requesting "Chicken" as Moog had. Soon she was kneeling on one of the too-high chairs, hungrily spooning hot soup into her mouth. She smiled over at Br'on, who was eating some kind of cheese soup. He smiled back. M'raj was eating something that looked like vegetable soup, and Moog had gotten himself a second helping. A few minutes later, all four friends were full for the first time in weeks.

Tika yawned. "Now that I'm full, I'm sleepy," she said. "But I sure wish I could have a bath first."

"No sooner said than done," announced Moog proudly. He helped her climb down from the chair, and then directed her through a door into a different room. Tika saw a bathtub, and felt tears spring to her eyes. Amazing how tender one could feel toward the possibility of hot water, she thought. She Sent, "Hot Water!" and was gratified to see the tub begin to fill with steaming water. Quickly assessing the height of the tub, and remembering the giant table and chairs, she Sent, "Half full". She didn't even notice Moog leaving the room or the door closing behind him.

Tika could have soaked for hours, but she felt guilty making her friends wait. She had discovered more drawers with bottles inside which turned out to contain lovely, scented shampoo and soap. When she was clean, though, she was reluctant to put her ruined clothes back on, and went searching. In a cupboard inside the room, she gratefully discovered clean clothes, however strange.

There were no dresses or tunics, as she wished. All of the garments, in fact, were odd, one-piece outfits, with the leggings attached to shirts. And white, of course. And way too big – she had to roll sleeves and legs up and up until they looked a bit silly. Still, it felt so good to be clean, and in clean clothes, that she didn't mind.

When she emerged from the bathing room, Br'on and M'raj were deep in conversation, and she had to clear her throat to get their attention. Their smiles when they saw her were amused, but neither elf said anything unkind.

"My turn!" announced M'raj, jumping up and running in before Br'on could protest. Then it was Br'on's turn, and finally Moog's, until all four elven were clean and dressed in the one-piece outfits from the cupboard.

"I can't believe how good it feels to be clean," said Br'on. "It's hard to imagine how I used to fight my mothers about taking a bath!" The other elveens smiled, and then Tika yawned, and Moog was once again able to play host and show the other three through yet another door into a room with dozens of beds – all white.

"Whoever those 'Media' were, there were sure a lot of them," said Tika in wonderment. They chose beds side by side to avoid feeling overwhelmed in the huge room.

"Now all I need is my SoulFather playing his violin, and I'll feel right at home," said Br'on with a smile.

"Okay, I'll try," joked Tika, Sending his request without the least belief it would be granted. So a moment later, when violin music filled the room, she screamed. Was there a ghost in the room?

"Thank-you, Tika," shouted Br'on over the music. "Now could you stop it, please? It doesn't sound the least like SoulFather Tem, and it's too loud."

Tika Sent again, and the music stopped. "Maybe the creatures who made this place were hard of hearing," she said, her ears still ringing. Anyway, Magik is sure strong in this place. Maybe we should just move everyone in the Village here."

But even thinking about it made all four homesick, and no one said anything else as they settled down to sleep. Tika Sent, "Lights out", and the room fell into darkness. She thought she would never sleep in such a strange place, but food, a warm bath, and a real bed worked their own Magik, and she was soon deeply asleep.

Chapter Twenty-Four: Battle

The next morning, over their breakfast of soup, the four elveens discussed how to get Proxy to open the doors. Tika had the most experience dealing with dragons, but it seemed little help, since the only time she'd almost gotten past Fyr'wall, she had found herself stopped by Proxy.

There seemed to be nothing to do but enter Vee'ar once more and try to reason with the dragon. She didn't seem hostile to them; if anything, she seemed to want to help, but was unable to get past her own rules.

"Remember the explosion?" asked Br'on before they entered the booths. "Maybe we could break the door down using that button on the carriage."

"Worth a try," agreed the others, so they got into the carriage and rode it to within a hundred yards of the door.

"I think you three should hide behind something," said Br'on as he prepared to press the button. "I'm not sure what will happen." So the other elveens got out and crouched down behind the carriage. Tika put her fingers in her ears, and closed her eyes. Moog couldn't resist peaking over the top of the carriage.

"Ready," he told Br'on.

Then Br'on pressed the button, and a burst of light flashed out from the front of the carriage, hitting the doors with a "Boom!" The air shook with the impact, but when all four elveens opened their eyes, the doors seemed unchanged. Br'on gestured to the others and they approached the doors, leaving the carriage behind.

Once they were close, they could see where the beam of light had hit. There was a dark circle on the face of one. But the door itself wasn't so much as dented!

Sighing with disappointment, the four elven turned and once more entered the booths. Slipping the metal ring over her head, Tika felt calm and happy, which seemed odd since they were no closer to their goal than they had been the day before. She put it down to being clean and well-fed.

"Access Source of Power," she began, and found herself facing the large, shiny red dragon.

"Hello, Tika Tamir," said Proxy. "Did you eat and sleep?"

"Yes, thank you," she answered politely, then felt her resentment rising. "How can you be so nice to us, yet not help us?" While she was speaking, the other elveens appeared beside her, and they, too, waited for an answer.

"As I told you yesterday, I have no algorithm," said Proxy.

"What does that mean?" asked M'raj.

"It means, I have no rule for dealing with beings such as yourselves."

"Who did you expect to deal with?" Tika asked.

"Humans with Authorization Codes," said Proxy.

"What are 'humans'?" Br'on asked.

"They are my creators. I am supposed to give Access to some of them, and no Access to most others. But I have had no request for Access for more than two thousand years. It seems there is no one left who can clarify your status."

"Who do you need to keep out?" asked Br'on shrewdly.

"Our enemies," said Proxy.

"Are we your enemies?" Br'on asked.

"I don't know," said Proxy. "That's the problem. I have no algorithm to use to make that judgment."

"Don't you know us from the Village?" asked M'raj.

"Yes, but that was there. It's different here. This place is Top Secret!"

"Could we give you the Knowledge you required?" asked Tika. "Then you could judge for yourself."

"The amount of Knowledge I require for decisions regarding Access is petabytes. . . . It would take probably the rest of your lives to answer all the questions I need answered, and you yourselves might not even know the answers to some of the questions. Perhaps no elven do."

"Such as?" demanded Br'on, insistent.

"Such as, why did your people come here? And from where?" said Proxy.

"The second one is simple," said Br'on. "The Village."

"No, I mean before that."

"There is no 'before that'," said Br'on. "We have always lived in the Village."

"No, you haven't," said Proxy simply. "Humans used to live there."

"What are 'humans'? And what happened to them?" asked Tika, though her head was spinning with the idea that elven had not always lived in the Village.

"Humans are – were, I guess – my creators. They were beings who lived on the planet for thousands of years." She gestured, and a screen appeared, hanging in mid air. On the screen flashed images of – creatures – similar to the female holo on their carriage. Like elven, they came in a variety of sizes and colors, but none possessed proper ears or eyes. It was a bit overwhelming. The elveens looked at each other but could think of nothing to say.

Finally, Tika spoke up. "So – they were taller than us, right?"

"Yes, overall."

"So – all of our buildings – windows and doors – are the height they are because they were designed for –hiu-mans?" Tika's stomach didn't feel very good. She was sorry she had eaten such a big breakfast!

"Yes. You – inherited – a world designed for – beings – much bigger than you."

"What does 'inherited' mean?" Moog asked.

Proxy gestured again and the screen disappeared. "Inherit is when you get things from your parents when they pass away. But in your case, you inherited the whole world."

"So – what happened to the humans who lived in our Village?" M'raj asked.

"I do not know for sure what happened to them," said Proxy. "That is part of the problem. Over a long period of time, humans Accessed Net less and less often, and then not at all."

"Did they die?" asked M'raj in a small voice. The hair on her arms and neck stood on end. This whole discussion made her very uneasy.

"I must believe so," said Proxy sadly. "I used to have other ways to gain Knowledge on the world, but over the centuries, all of them have failed as well. I have been blind here in Net for too long. That's why I'm glad you're here, and that's why I gave you the hint to lead you here. But I am restricted by the set of rules my creators gave me, and they won't allow me to open the doors without sufficient Knowledge."

"How do you define an 'enemy'?" asked Br'on.

"A person or group who desires to hurt or destroy my country," said Proxy.

"What's your 'country'?" asked M'raj.

"United North America," said Proxy.

"You mean the Valley?" asked Tika.

"Hundreds of Valleys," responded Proxy. "Plus other mountain ranges, plains, deserts, oceans and so on."

Tika glanced at M'raj, who nodded. Both of them were thinking about what M'raj had discovered about the world. They hadn't told Br'on or Moog about it because it hadn't seemed relevant.

Tika had felt small in the guest quarters, with the furniture way too large, but now she felt smaller than ever. Her whole *world* was only a tiny portion of Proxy's 'country'?

Tika burned with the desire to ask if there were elven in the other valleys, but Br'on spoke before she got the chance.

"Couldn't you give us a test?" he asked, thinking out loud. "I mean, no matter what Knowledge you have, you would still need to confirm that Knowledge somehow, wouldn't you?"

"A test?" said Proxy. "Hmmm, let me consider." And she disappeared.

The four elveens looked at each other. "A test is a good idea," said M'raj, smiling at Br'on. "I just hope she thinks of one we can pass."

Then Proxy was back, and she was the same size as the elven, instead of towering above them. "Fight me," she commanded. "If you defeat me, you gain Access. If you don't defeat me, I will lock you out of Net, and you will have to go back to your Village."

There was a funny feeling which made all four elveens look down at themselves. They were now dressed in metal outfits, obviously for protection. Each had a sword at their side. Br'on also had a bow and arrows, Tika a spear, M'raj a long, heavy staff and Moog a heavy metal ball covered in spikes, attached to a stick with a chain.

Without another word, Br'on strode forward, happy that he had no limp in Vee'ar, stringing arrows to his bow as he went. The arrows he unleashed simply bounced off the metallic dragon, however, and he quickly threw the bow away.

At the same time, M'raj threw her staff at the dragon. Tika came forward with her spear, and Moog swung the heavy ball toward the dragon's head. A battle ensued. Although all four knew they were not the dragon's equals, they were brave and desperate. Once, Proxy used her heavy tail to knock the spear from Tika's hand, just as she was about to stab the dragon with it.

As quickly as they could press forward the attack, the dragon countered it. Over and over again, Proxy sent one or the other of them flying with her powerful tail. Though sweating and out of breath, they refused to give up against their stronger opponent. Br'on rushed Proxy from behind, ready to swing his sword. But the dragon seemed to have eyes in the back of her head, for she turned and blew fire at the elf, making him jump and tumble out of the way.

Tika picked up her spear, though her right arm throbbed from one of the dragon's blows. She remembered killing the monster outside with a blow to its eyes, and aimed her spear there, throwing with all her might. Proxy grabbed the spear out of mid-air, and broke it in half, and then in half again, grinning as if she were enjoying the battle.

Tika wondered how much longer they could continue this way. To be truthful, her heart wasn't in it, anyway. What had Proxy ever done to deserve this?

Finally, Moog hit the dragon's shoulder with the ball, which stuck into her skin, making her groan. It seemed to disable her use of one of her arms, and Br'on saw an opportunity to press the attack.

He was about to swing his sword into Proxy's neck when he was knocked down from behind. Surprised, he rolled to see how the dragon had hit him, and instead saw Tika running past him to stand in front of Proxy, arms crossed.

"Stop!" she screamed. "All of you, stop!" She was crying. "I'm so sorry, Proxy," she said, pulling the metal ball from the dragon's red shoulder. "Perhaps I could Heal you."

"Keep fighting!" insisted Proxy angrily. "You are the only hope for your Village! Are you going to let them all down?" She bared her fangs at Tika, but the elveen had dropped her sword.

"You were trying to make us your 'enemies'," she said. "But we're not. We never wanted to hurt you. You tricked us into acting like an enemy. But we won't fight. There's nothing we need badly enough to kill you for. So you win. Go ahead, lock us out of Net." She turned to her companions. "Come on, guys, let's go home," she said. "I'm tired of tricks."

The four elveens found themselves suddenly out of Vee'ar, their metal rings gone dead. Slowly, they exited the booths, their faces slack with disappointment.

"I'm sorry, guys," Tika said to her companions. "I've let you down. But couldn't you see how wrong it was to fight Proxy? She'd done nothing but help us. We had no reason to hate or fear her. It would have been wrong to kill her, wouldn't it?"

The others had no argument for this, although Br'on, at least, was still excited from the fight and angry at Tika for quitting. They had been on the verge of victory, he felt sure. One more swing of his sword, and . . . What was the use? The battle was over. Net was dead to them. There was nothing to do but go back to the Village, and watch Magik continue to fail.

Moog, too, was silent. When they left the Village, all he had wanted was to turn back the clock and go back to the quiet and predictable life he had planned for himself. Since then, he had been hungry and tired, sore and bug-bitten, for the first time in his life. There had been days when he'd hated Tika, hated her quest, hated everything that forced him to survive so far from his beloved Village.

But by the time the battle had begun, though, Moog had realized he was a different elf. The fight had been as exciting as it was scary. He was tired; he hurt; but he wasn't done fighting, not by a long shot. He was shocked to see feisty Tika giving up. He thought he knew what she meant about not wanting to hurt Proxy, but he didn't see that they had had any choice. And now they were back to the beginning – worse than the beginning, because all they had to look forward to was the long walk home. He sat down, fighting back tears of frustration and disappointment.

M'raj alone seemed sympathetic to Tika, even if she, too looked disappointed and tired. "You're probably right," she said to Tika. "But where does that leave us?"

The other three elveens sat down beside Moog and closed their eyes. Was it to end like this?

Chapter Twenty-Five: Bill the GatesKeeper

A groaning sound made the four elven open their eyes, looking at each other to see who had made it. But it hadn't come from any of them. A short distance away, they could see the emerald green doors slowly opening!

They were on their feet in an instant, running toward the opening. The doors were more massive than the elven could have imagined. Not only were they thirty feet tall, and at least as wide, but when the four elveens began to pass through them, they realized the doors were more than ten feet thick. Who could have created such things?

Proxy's voice greeted them as they passed through the doors. "Welcome to Central Operations, for which your CenOps was named," she said.

"But – why?" Tika asked. "I thought we lost."

"Do you know what the difference is between a friend and an enemy?" asked Proxy's voice. "A friend is someone who will give up their own advantage, rather than hurt you." She paused, as if thinking. "I didn't really know that myself. I wasn't trying to 'trick' you into being my enemy, Tika. I meant the challenge to be genuine. I hoped that you would defeat me, and Coded Net to give you Access if you did.

"But you did something different, something I did not think of myself. You gave up what you needed so badly, rather than hurt me. That is a friend, I think. An enemy would not have done so."

The other three elveens looked at Tika in amazement. Giving up had been the right thing to do? They shook their heads. They would have to think about that later. Right now, there was a new place to explore.

If the cave-tunnel had seemed large, Central Operations was *huge*. And, thankfully, not all white, Tika noticed. She could not see a ceiling as far up as she could see, just rows upon rows of wooden railings. Did those indicate layers of rooms? So many, many rooms?

Throughout the central room were wooden boxes, tables, cupboards, and panels, upon all of which lights blinked. Tika felt dizzy again. It was too much to take in. She walked forward anyway, sensing the Line of Power led straight ahead. The others followed. Finally, she found herself in front of a circular table, with a number of chairs arranged around it. On the other side of the table stood a column with strange symbols moving up and down inside it, as if raining from the darkness above.

"If this is the Source of Magik in the Village, what's wrong with it?" she Queried.

Suddenly, a giant appeared between the column and the table.

"– Are you Proxy?" Tika asked, fear making her voice quaver.

"No," boomed the giant in stilted Elvish, "I am Bill, the GatesKeeper. How can I help you?"

All four elven put their hands over their sensitive ears and stared at him, terrified. Nearly twice as tall as even Br'on, this 'Bill' creature had the same deformed ears as the tiny holo on their carriage. His hair was thin, and in front of his small, too-close-together eyes, he had pieces of glass, attached to his head with what looked like metal wire. He was much less fearsome-looking than Proxy, though, even for a giant.

"Greetings, Billthegateskeeper," said Tika. Wha–who are you?"

Bill lowered his voice to a more comfortable level. "Call me Bill, please. I am a hologram of the Artificial Intelligence, or ay-eye as we say, that runs this center," said Bill. "So you've defeated Proxy?"

"Not exactly," said Tika. "We refused to fight her, and she said that proved we weren't enemies."

"Interesting. So, who are you?"

"I am Wizardelf Tika Tamir, Elf One of the D'inn-Tiriki-K'ah-Ch'anja parentgroup. This is Wizardelf M'raj Al'bani, Elf Four of the L'la-Sh'een-Werek-J'endo parentgroup. That's Wizardelf Moog Moe'bis, Elf Four of the G'lin-Parda-Nur'in-Kli parentgroup, and that's Br'on Lleyn, Elf Two of the Durak-Tem-Wrel-Ji'nka parentgroup," introduced Tika politely.

"Well, that tells me nothing," smiled the hologram. "Can you say that again more simply?"

"We're elven," said Br'on. "From the Village."

"Ah," said Bill, sitting down on a low chair which had suddenly appeared behind him, making him eye-height to the elveens, for which they were grateful. "Would that be Firewall's Village?" Bill asked, smiling.

"Yes," said Br'on.

"

you're the aliens," said Bill. "How interesting."

"Aliens?" said all four at once.

"Um, you know, beings from another planet? Non-humans?" said Bill. Their faces remained blank.

"Let's try again," he said. "You know that the place you call your Village used to be populated with humans – beings who looked like me – before you came here, right?"

"Yes, Proxy showed us that," said Moog. "What's that got to do with 'aliens'?"

"Oh, dear," he said. "I'll back up ... Do you know what planet you're on?"

"You mean, something like Proxy's 'country'?" asked Tika, confused at his strange words.

"No," said Bill, "this country is only part of the planet. There are many countries on the planet, many planets in the solar system, and many solar systems in the universe. Got it?"

"That's big, right?" said Br'on. "Very big?" His blue eyes were wide.

Bill shrugged, and smiled at them as if they were elflings. "Yes – Bron, is it? – Yes, it is. Very big."

Tika glanced at M'raj. She shrugged to show she didn't see how this was helping, either.

"We're here to fix the loss of Magik in our Village," Tika explained, ignoring his strange descriptions. "We followed the Line of Power here. How do we fix it? Do you know what's wrong with it?"

"Magic?" Bill asked. "What magic?" He looked like he had never heard the word before.

"Are there no elven here who speak Elvish?" asked Moog impatiently. This Bill creature didn't seem to understand anything. Moog felt overwhelmed and therefore angry. He knew Bill was talking down to them. "And what's wrong with your ears?" he added, deliberately rude. For once, his bushy orange eyebrows looked threatening rather than comical.

Bill reached up and touched his ears thoughtfully. "You're right, Moog, my ears are quite different . . . I rather like yours, really. They move about so much, sort of like a dog's."

Moog couldn't stand the insult. "We're not animals, Bill," he said using the same fatherish tone Bill had been using on them. "We're elven – we're Wizardelven! And we're not stupid or we wouldn't be here. Now, are you going to tell us what's wrong with the Source or not?"

Bill straightened up like an elfling who has been chastised by a Teacher. "I'm sorry," he said, "it's been a long time since I talked with anyone other than the other ay-eyes here. I've gotten rude."

"Ay-eyes?" asked Tika

"Artificial intelligences. You see, a long time ago, I was a human – sort of like an – elf, only taller and with these different eyes and ears. I was very rich. When I knew at last that I was going to die, I had my personality uploaded into this computer. Others like me did the same thing. Now, it seems we are all that's left of humanity, and it's made us somewhat odd."

"*Uploaded*? Into a *what*?" said Br'on.

"Oh, I see," said Bill, rubbing his chin. "Um, you know what Net is, right?"

"Net is the source of all knowledge," said Br'on.

"Well, not exactly, Bron," said Bill, continuing to mispronounce his name as 'brawn', as if it was one sound instead of two. "Net is Knowledge stored in a computer . . . which is a machine for storing Knowledge."

"What's a – machine?" asked Moog. M'raj had returned to her silent state in the face of all of this strangeness.

"Oh, dear," said Bill, "this is going to be difficult. A machine is something manmade – I guess you would say elf-made – that does work so – peop – elven don't have to. You have machines in the Village, don't you? Stoves to cook your food on, and so on?"

"I – don't know. We cook on cookstones," answered Moog. "Are they machines?"

"Oh," interrupted Tika, excited. "I'm beginning to understand. Has this got something to do with the Dark Pieces inside of us, attached to the ladders?"

"Dark Pieces? Ladders? . . . Oh, yes. Nanos, exactly, Tika. I'm glad at least one of you understands," said Bill, relieved.

"But I *don't* understand, Bill," said Tika. "What are the Dark Pieces?"

Bill sighed, but explained slowly, as if talking to an elfling. "A machine is a – tool – but with moving parts, that uses electricity – Power – to do jobs that – elven don't want to do … How do you wash your clothes?"

What a strange question! "We put them in water, and scrub them along a rough board with some soap, and then rinse them out and hang them to dry," said Tika. "Why? How do – did – YOU wash clothes?"

"Well, Tika, what you're doing sounds like how humans used to wash clothes thousands of years ago. Eventually, we made machines that would wash our clothes for us."

"So a machine is like a servant?" asked Moog. "We don't have servants, but I read about them."

"Yes, exactly!" said Bill, happy. "It's a mechanical servant – sort of a smart tool. Are you following me so far?"

They were actually quite confused, but didn't want to say so, so they just nodded, and Bill continued. "A long, long time ago, more than two thousand years ago, in fact, humans started making machines smaller and smaller. 'Nano' means very, very, very tiny. Got that?" When the elveens nodded again, Bill continued. "We injected these tiny machines into our brains to make it easier to communicate with Net. Another way we used the Nanos was to communicate with appliances, turn on lights, and so on. Do you do that?"

"We use Magik to do that," said Moog. "A Hex."

"A Hex? You mean, like a magic spell? Can't be. There's no such thing as magic, Moog … Now let me think. . . . Oh, I think I understand. Hexadecimal is the language humans used to talk to computers. 'Hex' is probably a short form you learned from Net about how to communicate with your homes."

"It works with animals, too," said Tika, thinking wistfully of Blaize and hoping she was okay.

"Yes, we injected domestic animals such as horses, goats and sheep, with Nanos, just as we engineered humans with Nanos to make communication easier. – Can you talk to each other inside your heads?"

"If we Send – I mean, if we try," said Tika. "Not every thought gets Sent."

"Be confusing if it did, wouldn't it?" said Bill. "Well, that's all done through nano-machines inside of you – though, how did the nanos ended up inside of you aliens? – But never mind that now. Your homes have nano-communicators in them as well. The Dark Pieces inside of your brain talk to your home's machines, and they do what you tell them. It's nanotechnology, not magic."

Tika felt dizzy. She was grateful that she had been at least partially right, but this was too much to take in. *Not only was there no Magik, but elven had apparently not even been the ones to develop the tek-no-lo-gy!*

She forced herself to focus on their reason for being here. "But what has that got to do with the Lines of Power?" she asked.

"Well," said Bill, "the machines in your homes require energy to work, like your bodies need food. As the power has weakened, the machines don't run as well. Make sense?"

It did make sense to Tika. It explained how the patterns of the Lines of Power seemed similar to those on the Dark Pieces. It explained how the weakening of Power along the Lines meant Magik – or rather, tek-nol-o-gy, she realized – wouldn't work as well. Her stomach didn't feel well. No such thing as Magik? Was she, after all, an ordinary elf?

"So, are YOU a machine?" she asked finally.

"Yes and no, Tika," said Bill. "I am not sure I am the same being as the human who uploaded his personality, but I am both more and less than a machine. I depend on a machine – the computer – for my existence, much as you depend on your body. But I am capable of far more than just computing. While programs like Firewall and Proxy are limited by their algorithms – rules – I am constantly changing and growing, more like a – an elf."

"If you depend on a – machine – for your life, doesn't that mean the loss of Power is a serious problem for you, too?" asked Br'on. Tika looked at him, surprised. She'd worried that they'd left him behind in the conversation somewhat, but now she saw that he was keeping his focus where it should be.

"Yes, Bron, the loss of power is a problem for me, too," said Bill, turning to look at him as if he could really see out of his hologram eyes. "But it's been quite gradual and, as you may have noticed, it's not as bad here as it is in your Village. I don't think it's quite critical yet."

He seemed nonchalant, which puzzled Br'on. "Won't you die when the Power's gone?" he asked.

"Yes, I suppose so, but I've calculated that might be centuries from now. I've been experimenting with new robots to try to fix the problem, and thought I would probably come up with a solution in time."

"What exactly is wrong with the power?" asked Moog, not wanting to be left out.

"As far as I can tell, a meteor shower destroyed a number of the solar panels which are the source of our energy. They're on the space station and the robots there don't have the resources they need to build new solar panels. I have used robots down here to build new solar panels, but the robots so far aren't capable of getting them up there. . . . My hands aren't real, that's my trouble," Bill finished, looking at his hands and sighing.

The four elveens had understood almost none of what Bill had just said, except that he was unable to fix the problem because his holo-hands weren't real. Tika looked at Bill's hands carefully for the first time. She was horrified to see four stubby fingers and a thumb, instead of the normal three long, graceful fingers and a thumb that elven had. She looked at her own hands. Then Tika looked at Moog, Br'on and M'raj, and saw that they were thinking what she was thinking.

"Our hands are real," she said cautiously. "Could we help fix your 'solarpanels', or whatever?"

Bill looked happy for the first time since they'd met him.

"You know, that might just work," he said, sizing them up. "You're kind of small, but from what I've gathered, you're brave and strong." The elveens' ears blushed at the praise.

"We'd have to adapt space suits and so on," Bill continued. "But why not? As you say, your Village needs the power at least as much as I do." He was rubbing his hands together excitedly, a gesture comfortingly familiar to the elven. It was the first time he had seemed Elvish to them.

Then his face fell. "Oh, my!" he said. "Where are my manners? I have a – Message – for you from your ancestor, one of the original beings to come to this planet. Would you like to see it?"

"Yes!" said all four elveens at once.

"Hang on, just a sec … There," said Bill, and he was replaced by a lovely Elf who was wearing strange clothes.

"Greetings, my people," she began in old-fashioned Elvish.

"Greetings," began Tika, Moog, M'raj and Br'on together, but the Elf didn't react.

"Oh, it's another Holo," whispered M'raj into Tika's ear before turning back to listen.

"My name is Captain Sh'reen Tamir of the Skyship Ziton. Welcome! You must have many questions about our people and this new planet. I'll be happy to tell you as much as my programming allows."

"Tamir!" said Tika. That's my –" But before she could say the next word, the Captain disappeared and Bill was back.

"Sorry," he said. "It didn't occur to us to make Sh'reen into an ay-eye. This avatar isn't interactive at all. You can't ask her questions. She's basically just a recording. She'll just keep repeating her message."

"Oh, you mean like the holo on the front of our carriage," said Moog. "The one who told us about the Bunker."

"The – pardon?" Bill's eyes went back and forth at a dizzying speed for a moment. "Oh, you mean the Welcome holo on the Transport Cart … Yes, basically the same as that. But if you give me a bit of time, I can upgrade the Captain to a full ay-eye, and she will be able to give you any information about your people that is stored in Net. Is that acceptable?"

Tika wanted to know everything right now, but glancing at the others, whose ears were bent sideways with anxiety, she realized that they all needed some time to absorb what they'd heard already. So she said, "Yes. How long will it take?"

"Why don't you go back to the Media Quarters, eat, drink, and rest for a few days," Bill suggested. "Relax. You've had a hard journey. When the Captain is ready for you, I'll let you know. Then maybe, together, we can solve all of our problems."

Tika turned to leave, but M'raj placed a restraining hand on her arm. "One more thing before we go," she said to Bill. "Is there some way we could Access Net to contact our friends and families in the Village to let them know we're okay? It's too far to Send."

"Of course!" said Bill. "Sorry I didn't think of it earlier. Net here can be linked to your Net. I'll give you Access to your Net, and you can either leave a message there for someone, or if someone happens to be on while you are, you can talk to them yourself. There's a Com Station – uh, a Net Access place – in the rooms where you're staying. I'll key your Access for there. Okay?"

"Okay," said all four at once, unable to believe this was all happening. They were going to be able to talk to their parentgroups and friends, tell them about their journey, and what they might be able to do to fix the Power!

As the other three turned to leave, Tika said, "You go ahead. I want to ask Bill a couple more questions."

Chapter Twenty-Six: Pursuit

The other elveens must have been more shaken up than they appeared, because they agreed without arguing, and a few moments later, Tika was alone with the hologram.

"What can I do for you?" Bill asked, his face kind.

"I – We – It's just that, we have always believed in Magik, and now you're telling us that it isn't Magik, it's hiu-man tek-no-lo-gy … If the machines are basically invisible, what's the difference?"

Bill looked thoughtful, but before he could answer, Tika heard Proxy's voice inside her head, shouting "RUN!!"

"Where?" she Sent. She felt a hand try to grasp her arm, but she pulled away and sprinted forward without thinking.

"Left!" Proxy said, and Tika veered left.

"Tika Tamir!" said Xinar's voice from behind her. "Stop right now!"

Xinar! Of course he would have followed them in here. And they had unwisely failed to instruct Proxy to close the giant metal door! Tika sped up. Tika was sure she could outrun Xinar – but what if he had brought his apprentices with him? She was afraid one of them would do the Sleep Hex on her!

"Stairs!" commanded Proxy's voice, and sure enough, down a short hallway to the left was a set of metal stairs.

The stairs wound upward in a spiral, so Tika had the chance to see who was pursuing her. Sure enough, Xinar had stopped at the bottom of the stairs, but two apprentices – Sh'ila and Nik, she thought their names were, were close enough behind her to almost grab her! Darn her small stature!

"Right!" Proxy commanded as Tika reached the top of the stairs. "DUCK!"

C.A. MAVEN

Tika crouched, and the rope that had been thrown to catch her sailed over her head. She didn't have time to gloat, though, for a hand grasped her ankle as she tried to start forward again. She kicked backward as hard as she could, and heard a grunt and then a scream as one of her attackers fell backwards down the metal stairs.

She didn't have time to look as she leapt to her feet again and raced toward the right, along a narrow hallway lined with doors.

"Fourth door on your right. Go in and I'll lock it," said Proxy.

A moment later, Tika grabbed the door handle and rushed into the room, slamming the door against the fingers that tried to grasp her though the narrow opening.

There was another scream, and the hand withdrew. Tika was able to close the door. She heard it lock. She realized that she was shaking from head to foot, and sat down on the floor without looking around the room.

She was safe for now, but she was trapped! Tears sprang to her eyes. Would this nightmare never end?

"Tika?" It was Bill's voice and it sounded concerned but gentle.

"Yes, Bill?" Tika wiped her eyes on her sleeve and turned to see where he was. She was in a meeting room similar to the Council Chambers back home. There was a long table with a number of chairs around it. The back wall of the room was like the screens in CenOps, and on this screen, she saw Bill. He appeared to be sitting in a comfortable chair in the living room of a cottage. Tika had to remind herself that he wasn't real.

"Sorry, I can't project my hologram into this room," said Bill, leaning forward. "Are you okay? Who are those people, and why are they chasing you?"

Tika climbed into the chair closest to her before responding. "The – older elf is Xinar. He used to be a Wizardelf like me – like us – but his status was removed."

Bill was silent, and Tika wondered if he had heard or understood her. After a moment, though, he said, "Oh, I see. I have accessed the security records from your Village. This Xinar – seems – obsessed with you – or at least, your Power – though I still don't quite understand what you elven mean by this."

Tika sighed. She was tired, and hot, and still shaking. She wasn't up to explaining about Magik right at the moment. She didn't know what to say.

"Can you – hold them – somewhere where they can't hurt me – or us?" she asked instead.

"This has been done," said Bill after another hesitation. "Perhaps you should speak to him now?"

"Must I? … Can I have some water?" Tika said.

"There is a food port to your left," said Bill.

She turned and saw a small door in the wall, similar to the one in the Media Center. "Water" she said, and there was a beep. When she got down and went over to open the door, there was a strangely-shaped container of water there. "Thanks," she said, though she wasn't sure who she was saying it to. The water was cool and fresh, and helped her calm down as soon as she had taken a few sips. She turned back toward the screen, climbing back into her chair.

"I'm trying to understand what is happening," said Bill. "I don't want to be perceived as showing favor to you over him until I establish if he is a danger to me – or this facility – as well."

"Fine – but –" Before Tika could complete her sentence, the screen split, and showed Bill on the left, and Xinar and his apprentices on the right. The two apprentices appeared to be receiving medical treatment – from a monster – a *robot*, she reminded herself – similar to the one they had confronted outside the cave!

"Tika Tamir!" shouted Xinar, apparently seeing her on a screen as she was seeing him. "Let me out of here. You have no right to make me a prisoner!"

"I am the one who has limited your freedom for the moment," said Bill calmly. "Perhaps you could explain why you were attacking Tika?"

"This – elfling! – is overstepping herself. She is not here as a representative of the Village – but instead, as a rebellious elveen who refuses to listen to older and wiser elven." Xinar spoke with authority, and Tika shrugged to show that what he was saying was basically true.

Bill gazed at Tika in silence for a moment before looking at Xinar again. "I can see that she is much younger than you, but if she was able to trace the Line of Power back to this operations and generating station, then perhaps she is wiser than you credit her for," he said calmly.

"So why IS the power failing?" Xinar demanded. "I DO represent the Village, and we ask you to fix it, right now!"

Bill sighed, resting his hands on his knees. Then he looked at Tika again. "Why don't you ask HER?" he said to Xinar. "As far as I can tell, she is the only elven who actually understands anything about our technology." He nodded, encouraging Tika to speak.

"I TRIED to explain about the Dark Pieces and the Lines of Power, but nobody believed me," she said. "Especially you, Xinar, who don't represent the Village any more than I do, because you are actually a disgraced Wizardel –"

"Quiet, elfling!" shouted Xinar. "I will let the avatar speak to me." He looked at Bill. "What are you? You don't look Elvish."

Glancing at the screen, Tika saw that Bill looked frustrated, and he didn't answer Xinar. "Is he going to let up?" he asked Tika.

"Don't believe anything this elfling says! Tell me how to restore Magik to the Village!" demanded Xinar.

"There is no such thing a magic," said Bill softly. "What you call magic is actually mechanical – machines. Your cookstones are machines, and you use tiny machines inside your bodies to communicate with them. It's called technology."

"Heresy!" screamed Xinar. "Insanity! No such thing as Magik! As IF!"

Xinar's image disappeared from the screen. "Enough of HIM for the moment! … Can you explain more about who he is and why he attacked you?" Bill asked. "And what did he mean when he called you a 'rebellious elveen'?"

So Tika was forced to tell him the whole story, including how Xinar had Elfnapped them and, as a consequence, lost his Wizardelf title and Super'vis authorization. She explained how the Council had refused permission for this journey and how she – and her companions – had decided to set out anyway. "It's my fault that the others are here," she said, in case Bill decided to keep her locked up, too. "They came, basically, to help me in a quest they knew no one could talk me out of."

"Will your – parentgroup – be angry when you contact them?" asked Bill. "Children – I mean, elflings – often rebel against their parents."

"I wasn't exactly rebelling against my parentgroup," she said. "I left without telling them because I didn't want to take the chance that they would say no … No elf has ventured so far from the Village in our history, as far as I can tell."

"Well, Proxy – and Fyr'wall – tell me that you did try to solve the problem from within your Village," said Bill. "But that they didn't have the authorization to answer your questions. They were put in place to protect the secret of this place, in case anyone wanted to destroy it. We – didn't think that it might also mean that no one would be able to find us to HELP us, either."

He was quiet for a moment before he spoke again. "So, what should we do with Xinar? He seems mentally unstable, and is obviously a danger to you."

"I really don't know," said Tika. "I guess, now that I'll be able to contact the Village, I can ask the Elders for their advice."

"That sounds wise," agreed Bill. "Now. You look exhausted. Why don't you join your friends, get cleaned up, have something to eat, and contact your Village? There will be lots of time for me to answer your questions."

As he spoke, Tika realized how right he was. She had been too scared to be tired, but now that the danger was past, she felt like she could fall asleep on her feet! Still, that would have to wait. Talking to her family came first!

Chapter Twenty-Seven: What to Tell?

M'raj was just opening the door to the Media Quarters as Tika arrived in the transportation that she had discovered was called a hovercart.

"Tika! What happened! You look awful!" M'raj said.

"Xinar, what else?" Tika said, and gestured for them both to go inside so Tika could tell the story to the whole group.

When she had finished, she had to stop Br'on from leaving to confront Xinar. "That snake!!" he cried. "I'll knock his teeth out!"

"Please, Br'on, let's worry about him tomorrow," said Tika, her voice tired. "I just want to talk to my family and then go to bed!"

"That's the other problem," said Moog. "How do we try to explain to our families about Nanos and Magik?"

"What's the difference, really?" said Br'on. "Whether it's 'Nanos' or Magik, it works the same. Right?" He looked at Moog for confirmation.

Instead of answering, Moog brought up another problem. "What about us not being the first to live in the Village?" he asked. "What about us being 'aliens'? Do we tell them that?"

"What about Bill? Do we tell our families about him – about 'humans'?" asked M'raj.

They were all silent for a moment, each looking down at their hands. Hands so unlike the 'humans', just as their eyes and ears were.

"Let's not say anything about any of that just yet," said Tika finally. "Let's just tell them we're alive and well, and that we're going to stay here awhile longer to try to solve the problem. We can ask them what we should do about Xinar. – But ... I think . . . the rest of it can wait until we're home again, and have asked the advice of the other Wizardelven."

Moog, Br'on and M'raj nodded their agreement, and the four friends went to Access Net together.

Tika was feeling a mixture of fear and excitement. It seemed silly, now that she was here, that she had ever thought that the solution would be as simple as tracing the string to the other end. From the sounds of it, they still had an enormous amount to learn and do. But that was exciting, too! She loved learning – and it felt as if she had been born for this adventure. She thought about the three elveens who had come through so much to be here with her – and realized that she wouldn't have it any other way.

***

The End

A Bit About Me:

I wrote my first short story when I was seven years old. While in university, I wrote a weekly humor column for the *McMaster Silhouette* newspaper, and was invited to publish a bit of my poetry. Later, I scored a job as the Regional Reporter for a group of weekly newspapers in Hamilton, Ontario, Canada. I have self-published a number of books which are available on Amazon in most regions. As a mother of three, I have had a lot of experience making up stories to entertain my kids.

I'm also a visual artist who sells paintings and upcycled home décor items. I have just started illustrating my own books, using a digital collage technique.

Since most of my stories and paintings come to me in dreams, I never really know WHAT I'll do next. Regardless of the genre, though, I want my work to promote acceptance of diversity.

Thanks for reading!
- Catherine

Catherine Maven.com

@catherinekatemaven   Catherine Maven
                       Writings & Poetry

www.ingramcontent.com/pod-product-compliance
Lightning Source LLC
Chambersburg PA
CBHW051502170626
46811CB00002B/597